CW00455587

Murder on Opening Night

A Myrtle Clover Cozy Mystery, Volume 9

Elizabeth Spann Craig

Published by Elizabeth Craig, 2018.

MURDER ON OPENING NIGHT

First edition. June 1, 2018.

Written by Elizabeth Spann Craig.

In memory of Amma.

CHAPTER ONE

"I'd no idea you were such a theater buff, Myrtle." Miles eyed the ticket that Myrtle brandished in front of her as if it were a poisonous snake.

"I'm not. But this is a freebie. Who can resist a freebie? These tickets are free and by-golly, I am going to use them!" Myrtle's voice was fervent with emotion as she waved the tickets in the air like someone who'd just won the lottery.

"How did you come about these tickets again?" Miles had every appearance of someone who'd planned on spending a quiet evening at home and was peeved that his plans had been hijacked.

"From Elaine," said Myrtle. Elaine was married to Myrtle's son, Red. "She volunteers at the community theater, but they couldn't make tonight's production. Their babysitter fell through," said Myrtle.

"I thought *you* were their babysitter."

"Their *other* babysitter," said Myrtle with the patient tone of someone who was dealing with a rather dense child. "The one that's unreliable. I offered to step in, but Elaine said she was just as happy to have an early night."

Miles said, "What's the name of this production? It's nothing fanciful, is it? I haven't been in the mood for something fanciful for quite a while."

"It's not *Midsummer Night's Dream*, Miles." She squinted at the ticket. "It's something called *Malaise*."

Miles made a face. "That sounds ominous."

"I'm convinced that *you've* got malaise. I've never seen anyone so reluctant to enjoy an evening out. Never mind, I'll find someone else to go with me. The problem with you, Miles, is that you've gotten too accustomed to lowbrow entertainment. Your soap opera watching has corrupted your taste."

"You're the one who got me hooked on the soap!" said Miles hotly.

"Only because *Tomorrow's Promise* provides a fascinating slice-of-life study. I know the characters in soap operas are caricatures, but they hit home so very often. We're all driven by passions." She paused meaningfully. "You're driven by the passion to organize your pantry alphabetically, which is likely what you'll be doing tonight instead of going out. It's all right. I'll introduce Wanda to a bit of culture."

Perhaps the bit about organizing his pantry hit too close to home. Or perhaps Miles simply didn't want to imagine Wanda at the community playhouse. It would have been a stretch for Wanda, Myrtle had to admit. Wanda didn't have an operational car. Myrtle would have to pick up the psychic and Myrtle didn't have a car, herself. Then there was the fact that Wanda may not be able to endure an entire production at the community theater without a cigarette. Wanda tended to agitate Miles and had done so since he'd discovered they were cousins. The resulting sense of responsibility had proven ... expensive ... for Miles.

Whatever his reasons were, Miles suddenly accepted Myrtle's invitation with alacrity. "Fine, yes. A night out. Okay."

"I'm bowled over by your enthusiasm," drawled Myrtle. "Shall we say seven-thirty tonight? Can you pick me up then?"

"If I'm not too busy clearing out my sock drawer," muttered Miles. He sighed. "This conversation has reminded me that there's something I need to talk to you about."

"What's that?"

"So ... I know Puddin drives you crazy," he said, referring to Myrtle's housekeeper.

"Is the sky blue?"

"Would you be at all interested in firing Puddin and hiring someone else?" asked Miles.

Myrtle stared at him. "Well, naturally. But you know as well as I do that I'm stuck with Puddin like a bad marriage. If I lose her, I lose Dusty. And I can't lose my yardman because he's the only one who'll mow and use the string trimmer around my yard gnomes. He and Puddin are a package deal."

Miles said, "I know. I noticed your gnomes are out in full force in both front and back yards. What did Red do wrong this time?"

Myrtle believed Red was a good son, except for the fact that he had a nasty habit of overstepping his boundaries. When he did, she lugged out her tremendous collection of garden gnomes. He loathed them—all the better to put them on display in her front yard where he could see them from his house across the street.

"He implied that I shouldn't drive after dark. Very ageist of him. Especially since my eyesight is far sharper than Red's failing vision," said Myrtle, sounding huffy.

"But surely that argument is completely hypothetical. You don't even have a car," said Miles.

"Still, it was completely out of line. It was an insult punishable by gnomes. And perhaps even more punishment is required. I might have to resort to calling Red by his legal name instead of his nickname."

Miles's eyes opened wide. "You mean he has another name?"

"Of course he does! Who names their baby 'Red?' No, in the South we hand down our ancient family names, even if it means that the child must go by a nickname to avoid being teased at school. It's tradition," said Myrtle.

"What is Red's name then? The one that would have gotten him teased?" asked Miles.

"Horace. He's the ninth Horace in a row. It was practically mandatory that he be named it," said Myrtle. "Otherwise, I'd have been haunted by the ghosts of Horaces past."

"Lucky for him he had red hair and an instant nickname," muttered Miles.

"I think that anyone named for a Pilgrim doesn't have room to talk," said Myrtle with a sniff.

"Miles Bradford wasn't a Pilgrim," said Miles stiffly. "Myles Standish was. William Bradford was. Myles Bradford, as a Pilgrim, is a figment of your overactive imagination."

Myrtle ignored this. "But going back to the original thread of our conversation. Who did you have in mind to replace Puddin? Although, of course, *anyone* would be better than Puddin."

Miles cleared his throat. "Wanda."

"*Wanda*!"

"Yes. She showed up at my house yesterday. She required ... financial assistance," said Miles.

"Showed up at your house? Please tell me she drove one of those decrepit vehicles," said Myrtle.

"No, the cars are all still up on cement blocks. I'm afraid she walked the whole way. Took her all day."

Myrtle put a hand to her head. "I can't believe it. Not again. No wonder she's stick thin. So this time she actually asked for money? She doesn't usually do that."

"She didn't ask for a dime. She asked me to help her find a job. Wanda said she was tired of the ceaseless struggle for survival," said Miles.

Myrtle raised her eyebrow. "*Wanda* said this?"

"Those weren't her exact words. I'm translating for her. She said something along the lines of: *ain't got no money and I'm sick of it.*"

Myrtle nodded. "Got it. But what is Wanda qualified to do?"

They mulled this over for a moment in silence. Miles said, "She does run her own small business."

"Fortunetelling out of one's home isn't like being a CPA or something," said Myrtle. "I don't think we can foist her on some hapless business as an office manager, if that's what you're thinking."

Miles said, "How about the housekeeping then? I know ... not for you. But for somebody else? Surely she must be qualified to scrub."

"I think she could do it, if she had to. But it's hardly second nature to her. I'm not sure she's an expert in spotting and eliminating clutter and grime. Think of the shack where she and Crazy Dan live. I wouldn't use the word 'tidy' to describe it."

Miles held up his hands in surrender. "I give up. What do you think she's qualified for?"

"I'd look at her gifts and interests," said Myrtle. "In other words, her sorcery."

"I'm not sure how that would fly in a corporate environment," said Miles. "Unless we send her to work at the stock exchange."

Myrtle snapped her fingers. "I know. Of course! The horoscope for the paper. Sloan, my editor, has been bellyaching for ages because we can't keep a writer for it. Wanda will be perfect!"

"Except, of course, for the fact that Wanda is illiterate," said Miles.

"I can fix that," said Myrtle.

"You can teach Wanda to read and write?" asked Miles doubtfully. "I know you're a retired English teacher, but Wanda would be a challenge. Even for you."

"No, I mean that I can edit whatever she writes. I'll get her to submit horoscopes for the paper in advance, and I'll clean them up really well. It'll be fine. And it certainly suits her the best," said Myrtle.

"Won't you have to run it by Sloan first?" asked Miles.

"He'll just be relieved to have it taken care of. But sure, I'll bring her with me to the *Bradley Bugle* office one day. I'm sure Sloan will go for it," said Myrtle.

"I'm glad that's taken care of. I'll drive out to see Wanda this afternoon and let her know. But right now, I'm famished. Is it all right if I make lunch for us while I'm here?"

Myrtle nodded thoughtfully, sitting down carefully into an armchair. "Of course. Although it might entail some creativity from you." Myrtle had the feeling that the cupboard was looking barren.

Miles bumped around in the kitchen for a few minutes. He opened the pantry and closed it. Opened the fridge and closed it. "There's a small amount of peanut butter," he called out. "But no jelly."

"It *is* possible to eat the one without the other," observed Myrtle. Although it did make for a very mucky meal.

There were more rummaging sounds. "No ham," he reported.

Myrtle sighed.

"But there is a bit of turkey," said Miles, sounding excited.

"Well, for heaven's sake, use that then."

A moment later, he peered solemnly from the kitchen door at her. "I would. Simply because I'm that hungry. But there's no mayo in your fridge. And you've got no bread."

"Miles, you should go on the stage, yourself. I've never heard such drama through a play by play forage for food. Let's give up. It sounds as if we're at the stage where we'll be eating stray pickles and various condiments if we continue. Red is taking me to the store later today, anyway and I'll stock up. In the meantime, let's go to Bo's Diner. We can pick lunch up and bring it back here." Myrtle caught the glance that Miles directed to her television. She quickly added, "And we won't miss a second of the soap, because it's all set to record."

THEY'D DECIDED MILES should drive to the diner. Unfortunately, parking was scarce at the popular lunch spot. There were no empty spaces on the street so Miles tried his luck around the back of the diner. They discovered that cars were even double-parked and parked in makeshift spots. Muttering, he drove down Main Street a ways more until he found an empty space. Myrtle was positive it would have been quicker to have walked from her house.

The diner was packed on the inside, too. When they walked through the door, they had to hover right there since the entire front of the diner was full of customers.

"We should have called for take-out," said Miles glumly.

"But then we'd have had to carry those greasy bags back home and *we'd* have ended up greasy, too. It's okay, Miles. People are in and out here. We'll soon get a table."

A blonde waitress wearing an excessive amount of eye make-up sauntered over. She immediately refuted Myrtle's statement. "Hey, y'all. It's going to be a forty minute wait, sugar. You okay to stand that long?" Her mascara-encrusted eyes were doubtful.

Miles said, "Actually, we'd rather order it for takeout and wait. That won't be as long, will it?"

"More like fifteen minutes, love."

Miles looked questioningly at Myrtle. She snapped, "I think I can stand for fifteen minutes without keeling over! For heaven's sake."

The waitress nodded and poised a pen over a battered ordering pad. "What'll you have?"

"A pimento cheese chili dog," said Myrtle promptly. "With fries."

As usual, Miles looked queasy when hearing Myrtle's order. His own was healthier. "The chicken salad platter with a side of fresh fruit."

"Got it. We'll get that right up for y'all," said the waitress, dashing off on impossibly high heels.

A middle-aged man who was sitting on the bench in the waiting area spotted Myrtle and leaped to his feet, gesturing to the seat he'd just vacated. Myrtle knew this was one of the few benefits to being in one's eighties, so she was quick to take advantage of it. Another middle-aged man stood up, looked at Miles, and gestured to *his* seat. Miles pretended not to see it, still being somewhat sensitive about his age—in Myrtle's mind, anyway. The man settled back down on the bench. The front door continued opening and more customers continued pouring in so Miles moved away from the door and stood near Myrtle.

Myrtle cocked her head to one side and listened intently for a minute. Then she tugged on Miles's khakis. "Miles! That table directly behind us is full of the actors and actresses from tonight's show!"

Miles squinted at them. "Are they practicing now? They seem very agitated."

"No, I think they're just arguing amongst themselves. You know how excitable these theater types are."

Myrtle and Miles listened in, Myrtle with her back to the table and Miles facing them. One of the actresses was speaking disparagingly about the cheap costumes and the problems with sound and lighting. An actor complained that he didn't have enough lines or stage time to make all the practices worthwhile.

Miles said in a wondering voice, "I'm bowled over that they're having this conversation and you and I are so obviously listening in. Do you think that's because they're so used to having an audience that they simply ignore it?"

"No, I think it's because you and I are old, Miles. They don't even see us. Welcome to being elderly. It's like having an invisibility cloak," said Myrtle.

Now Myrtle turned around too, to demonstrate her point. Conversation and quarreling continued as it had before. Myrtle saw a tanned young woman in a tight red mini-dress with brunette hair down to her hips say, "My problem isn't lack of lines. I've got so *much* stage time that it's hard to remember everything." She made a moue as if it were a huge burden to be such a star. But her eyes glinted with a malicious glee.

A thin woman who was about forty with red hair snapped at her, "You'd better remember them all or you're not going to go very far in this business. Don't think you can make it on looks and youth alone for very long."

The tanned young woman just gave her a sweet smile back. "I'll be right back. I've got to touch up my face." Although she didn't seem to be wearing makeup at all.

The redhead threw her balled-up napkin at the table. "That's it. I can't stand working with Nandina anymore. She thinks she's such a big-shot."

"She *is* a big-shot. She's the lead in the play," pointed out a studious looking young man with black framed glasses.

"She was miscast," gritted the redhead between her teeth. "The girl can't act her way out of a paper bag."

A thin girl with blonde hair styled in a pixie cut seemed to be repressing a grin. She wore a flowing top covered with psychedelic paisleys and appeared to be thoroughly enjoying herself. "Veronica, you should try playing one of your practical jokes on her. Like the one for the last play where you got Tina signed up on every junk mail list in the country. I bet she's *still* trying to dig out from under the catalogs!"

The young man in glasses said swiftly, "Veronica, you're just upset because you're not playing young female leads anymore. You should face the facts. You're simply too old to play those parts anymore."

Miles grunted at this. "She looks like a baby to me."

"Shut up, Skip," said a cool male voice. Myrtle peered intently at the back of the speaker. He had long blond hair, a muscular build, and was wearing a white sports jacket. Since his back was facing her, she couldn't see his face, but his whole aura was one of strength and style.

Skip raised an eyebrow in what appeared to be a practiced gesture. "You're standing up for Veronica? Since when, Blaine?"

"I'm standing up for every cast member," said Blaine briskly. "As for Nandina, it's easy to forget how it was when we were starting out, ourselves."

"Which has been longer ago for some of us than for others," noted Skip snidely.

Veronica rolled her eyes.

Then Myrtle observed that the eyes of the vast majority of male diners were trained in one direction. She turned to see the young woman, who was apparently Nandina, sashaying toward the table. She was walking with fluid movements—using almost a runway walk—as she went. A faint smile played around her lips as she felt the eyes on her. She sat in the booth next to Blaine.

Nandina turned to a silent and watchful man on the other side of the table and gave him a simpering smile. "Roscoe, you've been so quiet that I didn't even know you were here. Tell me, how *is* Josie doing? I haven't spoken with her for so long! I'll have to give her a call today. And this time, I'm really going to do it instead of just putting it off."

Roscoe flushed a mottled red and shot Nandina a look of unadulterated fury. Miles raised his eyebrows at Myrtle. For a moment, Myrtle wondered if the man with the dark, springy hair and beard were going to spring across the table and throttle the young woman. But instead he ignored her, finishing off the last bite of his food with a shaking hand.

Miles raised his eyebrows. He leaned over and said, "That Blaine seems to be friendly with Nandina."

Myrtle gave up on the entire premise of not listening in. The group of actors couldn't have cared less about Myrtle and Miles, anyway. She stood up and peered down. Sure enough, Blaine had a hand on Nandina's knee under the table. Myrtle noticed that the girl with the pixie style haircut also noticed and smirked.

Their eavesdropping was interrupted by the sugary voice of their waitress now belting out over the chatter, "Clover and Bradford! Takeout is ready!"

"Well, shoot," said Myrtle. "That was even better than *To-morrow's Promise*."

They quietly rode the short distance to Myrtle's with their greasy bags on the floor in the back of Miles's Volvo.

Myrtle finally said, "If the play tonight is half as interesting as lunch, then we should be in for a treat."

"There's a lot of tension and conflict going on with those people. If that translates over into the play, it might end up being a stressful experience," said Miles, pushing his glasses up his nose. He carefully parked in Myrtle's driveway and then grabbed the bags of food from the backseat floor.

"Did I forget to mention the best part about this community theater? It serves wine. And the audience is allowed to bring their drinks into the theater," said Myrtle as she unlocked her front door.

"Wine might be the saving grace of the evening," said Miles.

"Can you imagine working on a play with that constant sniping? How on earth do they learn their lines?" asked Myrtle. She walked into the kitchen and pulled out napkins and plates.

"The source of all the arguments was one person: that Nandina woman. She was obviously a real troublemaker." Miles put the food out on the plates and turned on Myrtle's television set.

Myrtle brought in two glasses of water. "That was clear, yes. Part of it was ego, but part of it seemed to be due to the fact that she loved the drama."

"Does she have top billing on the playbill?"

"I believe this may be the type of production that doesn't *have* a playbill, actually," said Myrtle, settling down in her favorite armchair.

Miles brought up the taped soap opera and Myrtle snapped her fingers. "Hold on a second, Miles. There's one more thing I forgot to do. Elaine mentioned that we get discounted tickets for the next production if we share on social media that we're going tonight."

"Pass," said Miles, holding up his hands in surrender.

"Well, I'm interested, even if you're not. Such a fuddy-duddy. I'll share it on Twitter," said Myrtle. She got back up and walked over to her desk. Miles started eating his chicken salad platter.

"I wonder if I say that Miles Bradford and I are attending, if it means that you can get discount tickets, too," murmured Myrtle.

"I said that I'd pass on it," reminded Miles. "Besides, if you share an update like that, the whole town will presume that we're dating." Myrtle was quiet, clicking around on her laptop. Miles sighed. "I suspect you're not listening to me again."

"Hmm? Sorry Miles, I was just looking at something online. I was going to mention the Bradley Community Theater in the update and I just saw they posted something rather interesting," said Myrtle, sitting down in the desk chair.

Miles ate some of his fruit cup. "What did they post?"

"It says: *Tonight's production features the better off dead Nandina Marshall.*"

CHAPTER TWO

THE AFTERNOON FLEW by for Myrtle. *Tomorrow's Promise* had actually been rather suspenseful with Sedate Homemaker Carrie brainwashed by Wicked Ethan into robbing a bank. The nap that Myrtle had planned on taking afterward hadn't taken place, because her mind was so busy thinking about the soap and the scene that Miles and she had witnessed at the diner. When her son, Red, showed up at her door at around five o'clock, she frowned ferociously at him, unsure why he was there.

Red, of course, was always quick to attribute any forgetfulness on Myrtle's part to the ravages of age. "Mama?" he asked. "Did you forget I was going to take you to the grocery store?"

Fortunately, Myrtle recovered quickly. "Certainly not. How could I forget when my cupboards are bare? No, I was simply stunned by your choice of attire, that's all."

She hid a smile as Red quickly glanced down at his clothing, allowing her time to calculate where she'd put her purse after she'd returned from the diner.

"Shorts and a golf shirt," he muttered, almost to himself. "What's wrong with what I've got on?"

"Oh, nothing. I suppose I've just gotten out of the habit of seeing you in short pants, that's all. Ordinarily, when you escort me to the grocery store, you're in your police uniform. It's sort of fun being squired around by someone in uniform."

"Next time I'll remember the fact that you're on a power trip," said Red with a sigh.

It was extremely unfortunate that the grocery excursion had slipped Myrtle's busy mind. She had no list to work from and no coupons from the paper. It was rare that she went to the store and paid face value for anything. Red knew this, too, and seemed determined in his best detective manner to ferret out the fact that his mother had indeed forgotten their foray to the store.

"Where's your list, Mama?" he asked as he pushed her cart up aisle one.

"In my head," she said with a sniff. "It's an excellent mental acuity exercise, if you haven't tried it."

"No, I need the crutch of a list. Too much going through my mind to remember what we're out of." He paused as Myrtle squinted at a shelf, grabbed a couple of things, and threw them in the buggy. "You usually have a bunch of coupons, too. Did the paper not deliver them this week?"

She'd have used that excuse if she could, but since Red knew everyone in town, he'd have asked her delivery person to give him coupons for her. Myrtle gritted her teeth. Her backup strategy was to purchase items that were on sale at the store. And then, of course, to pick up her regular staples of milk and bread since they rarely had coupons, anyway. Surely she could make a meal out of the store's weekly specials. However, this method involved a tedious trip up each aisle, peering at small yellow sales tags that the store placed on the shelves.

"I didn't need the coupons this week, as a matter of fact. It was an amazing thing. Everything I needed at the store was on sale in the grocery flyer." Myrtle reached for a bottle on the shelf. She decided a change of subject was in order to throw Police Chief Red off her scent. "I was wondering, Red, what you knew about this play."

"What play?" asked Red absently. He was staring at the contents of Myrtle's cart which now consisted of quite a few condiments, including a large bottle of barbeque sauce. "Planning a barbeque, Mama?"

Myrtle decided to ignore the question altogether. "The play that *you* were planning on seeing tonight. With Elaine."

Red watched as his mother put a jar of pimentos into the cart. And then a second jar. "Oh, that. Well, you know how Elaine gets fixated on these different hobbies and things. We've suffered through photography and knitting and painting. She's *very* talented, it's just that she hasn't really settled on a pastime that ... well, that showcases her talent."

"So her involvement with the community theater is a hobby then, like the others?"

"Not exactly. This time it's different. She realizes that she probably doesn't have the time to be part of the *cast*. That's a lot of practicing, and with my job, sometimes I'm not home at a predictable time. And Jack being so little and all ... you know."

His face brightened as Myrtle finally turned the corner to aisle two.

"Elaine is volunteering her time there, then," said Myrtle. "I see. So she's spending enough time to form an opinion of the cast."

Red had the uncomfortable look of someone who was being put to the test and realized a strong possibility that he might fail. "I suppose she would have, yes. Hey, I see these baked beans are on sale—want some baked beans?"

Myrtle was still trying to maintain the fiction that she was working off a mental list. "No, I don't need any baked beans, thank you. What does Elaine think of the cast of this current show?"

Red cleared his throat and seemed to be anxiously casting back in the recesses of his memory for any half-listened-to conversations. "Let's see. She did say that there was a woman there who was very obnoxious. Sort of a diva."

Probably Nandina. "Is she fighting with the rest of the cast?" Myrtle absently threw a can of early peas into her buggy, followed by another one.

"That's what I don't know. I only know she's making trouble." Red turned to give her a searching look. "Why are you so interested in the cast of this play? *You're* not making trouble yourself, are you?"

"Of course not. Miles and I were at Bo's Diner for lunch today and saw the cast eating there and squabbling like children. I wondered how much Elaine knew about them, that's all—considering that Miles and I are going to be watching the play tonight." Myrtle frowned at the shelf. It was difficult to pretend to be working off a mental list, figure out more about the cast members, and actually find low-priced food all at the same time.

"I'm sure, like with anything, the more time you spend with someone, the more opportunity you have to get annoyed by them." Red gave his mother a long-suffering look as if she were the perfect illustration of this concept. "Say, do you think we can move through the next aisle a little faster? At this rate, you'll be too late to even see the show tonight."

AT PRECISELY SEVEN-thirty, Myrtle's doorbell rang. She opened the door and blinked at Miles for a moment. "Miles! You're wearing a suit!"

"Naturally," said Miles stiffly. "We're going to the theater." He studied Myrtle's comfortable dark slacks, sensible shoes, and white tunic. "Aren't we? It doesn't look like you're ready to go. Didn't we say seven-thirty?"

Myrtle stood aside to allow Miles to step in. "This is community theater, Miles. There's no need to look that nice at any art venue in Bradley. I feel as if I'm being accompanied by a waiter."

Miles sighed. "I'll leave the jacket here."

"Can you leave the tie here, too?"

"Then I'd look silly," said Miles.

"I suppose we don't have time for you to change." Myrtle picked up her pocketbook and fished the tickets out.

"It won't take that long for us to get to the theater," said Miles reasonably. "I can make a quick change."

"But these are general admission tickets," said Myrtle, peering at them. "Pooh. I should have noticed that. Technically, we should already be in line to ensure a good seat."

Miles was looking less and less amused about their evening out.

Myrtle made a quick about-face in the interest of time. "Actually, you look very handsome. It's good to show respect for the actors and the production, isn't it? Let's head out. Otherwise, we won't even have time to grab a wine at the concession stand before going in."

Myrtle, never one to be late, was tense in the car on the way over. But as soon as they strolled into the small theater downtown, she started to relax. "There aren't so many people here. We should be able to get a good seat."

Miles muttered, "May have something to do with the name of the play. Malaise doesn't quite have the same ring to it as Fiddler on the Roof."

"Let's get that wine," said Myrtle.

A few minutes later, wine in hand, they entered the theater. They were able to sit on the second row. And, since the seats were arranged stadium-style, they could see the stage perfectly.

Miles studied the program. "There doesn't seem to be an intermission," he fretted.

"Well, that's all right, isn't it? The play will be over sooner." Myrtle watched the feet she could see under the small gap under the closed curtain on the stage.

"It's just that with all this wine, I'll have to visit the men's room," he sighed.

Myrtle switched seats with him so that Miles could sit on the aisle.

Right before the curtain went up, the theater owner, a Mr. Toucan, spoke a few words about the production and asked them to turn their phones off. He was a large man who wore an olive tie over a rather dingy khaki button-down shirt. He had orange hair and a matching mustache, and wore over-sized glasses and a pocket protector. "You're in for a treat tonight, ladies and gentlemen!" he promised.

"I don't think I know Mr. Toucan," murmured Miles.

"He used to own the pet food store," said Myrtle. "But apparently, owning a community theater has been his lifelong dream."

"Imagine that," said Miles in a stunned voice.

"We can't all be CPAs, Miles," said Myrtle reprovingly.

"Can't all be engineers, you mean. I was an engineer," said Miles in a tight voice.

"Same thing."

As much as Myrtle was determined to enjoy her arts outing, she had to admit that the play was odd. It opened with a flashback of some sort. Then most of the actors had asides with the audience, breaking down the fourth wall in a way that Myrtle found distracting. There was then a set change behind the curtain with very loud music accompanying it. When the curtain opened, the stage was set for a dream sequence, complete with actress Veronica doing some sort of dreamy dancing while actress Nandina "slept" on a bed on the stage.

Myrtle glanced over at Miles. He appeared to be engaged in a dream sequence of his own. Myrtle elbowed him and he awoke with a start. "You're missing it," hissed Myrtle.

"I liked the performance in the diner better," whispered Miles.

Myrtle frowned. "What's going on now?" she said.

Nandina appeared to have missed a cue. The actor that they knew as Skip was repeating loudly, "Good morning, darling," to a very still Nandina.

"Perhaps Nandina has fallen asleep, too," suggested Miles dryly.

Skip apparently suspected so, too. He walked over to the bed and seemed to improvise a little. "I know it's hard to wake up and face the day sometimes, dear, but we simply must, mustn't we?"

Miles made a face at the stilted dialogue.

Skip lightly touched Nandina's face. Then he abruptly dropped character and more roughly tugged her arm. Finally giving up all pretense of being in character, he said, "Nandina! Nandina!" He turned to look offstage. "She's not breathing!"

CHAPTER THREE

MR. TOUCAN APPEARED from the wings. He was wringing his hands. "Is there a doctor in the house?"

No one came forward.

"Engineering and teaching skills are never helpful in these situations," said Myrtle regretfully.

"Anyone?" pleaded Mr. Toucan. But apparently the entire house was composed of non-medical types. "Could someone lower the curtain, please?"

The volume of the audience rose in distressed murmurs. They seemed to be wondering if this were just a very avant-guard production or if something were genuinely wrong. Myrtle took out her cell phone and turned it back on. "I'm calling Red," she said grimly.

When Red picked up, Myrtle could barely hear him with all the commotion in the theater. Impatiently, she got up, grabbed her cane, and moved out to the small sitting area in front of the concessions.

"What's going on?" asked Red, sounding a bit exasperated.

"It's the play," said Myrtle.

"Not your fixation with this play again. You know I didn't plan on going there tonight, Mama. Besides, hasn't it already started?"

"It's started all right. But there was a plot twist that I didn't see coming. One of the actresses is unresponsive on the stage."

"*What*? It's not part of the show?"

Myrtle could hear sounds on Red's end that indicated that he was probably already getting dressed.

"It's a very odd show, but no—this isn't part of the storyline, I'm sure of it," said Myrtle.

"All right. Just hold on. I'll be there in five minutes," Red said grimly.

Myrtle hung up and watched as Miles approached the concessions stand, solemnly holding his plastic cup. "May I have more wine?" he asked the worker earnestly.

Red arrived in mere minutes and quickly stopped the hubbub in the theater. "Okay, I'm going to need everyone here to keep it down to a whisper," he barked as he climbed the few stairs to the stage and disappeared behind the red curtain.

The noise in the theater did drop and Myrtle could almost make out the murmurs on the other side of the curtain. A few minutes later, Red walked out looking grim. He addressed the audience again, saying, "There has been a tragic death here tonight. Under the circumstances, I'm going to need to call in a team from the state police. In the meantime, I'll need everyone to stay in their seats, or at least in the theater, until we have a chance to take statements."

"We'll be here all night," said Miles, looking slightly shell-shocked. He'd gone from accepting that he'd have an evening out to the realization that it was going to be a very long evening out, indeed.

"While we're here, this might be a good time to try to gather some information about what's happened," said Myrtle.

"In a gossipy way or an official way?" asked Miles. "Because I don't think we have any official clout, despite your being the mother of the police chief."

"I have plenty of clout as a crime reporter for the *Bradley Bugle*," pointed out Myrtle smugly.

"Crime reporter? You've got a helpful hints column, Myrtle."

"Sloan has asked me to contribute crime stories when I have the opportunity," said Myrtle.

"When *Tomorrow's Promise* isn't on?"

"When there's actual crime in Bradley," said Myrtle with a sniff. "Which doesn't happen all too often. There are only so many stories one can write about Cooter Carson's bar fighting proclivity. This, on the other hand, looks as though it might be murder. Poor lamb. She seemed to be a trouble-maker, but she was awfully young to die."

Miles nodded. "It does seem rather unlikely that someone of her age would suffer a natural death in these circumstances."

"Then let's find someone we can talk to. Someone who *isn't* behind that curtain," said Myrtle.

She and Miles looked around them. The play was hardly sold out, but there were a fair number of people in the audience.

None of them looked like anyone who'd know much about Nandina's death, though. Then Myrtle spotted someone.

"That young girl there. The one with the pixie haircut and the short floral dress. She was at the diner with the cast, wasn't she?" Myrtle squinted at the girl. She looked to be about twenty years old. She had a pointed chin and large eyes that combined with her haircut to make her look like a fairy.

Miles said, "I think so. She seemed to mostly be listening in to the conversation. Like we were."

"Then she's exactly the person we need to be talking to," said Myrtle. "Could you fetch her, Miles?"

Miles looked uncomfortable. "She'll probably think I'm some sort of weirdo or something."

Myrtle once again took in Miles's sensible tie, starched button-down shirt, dark pants, and silvery hair. "Unlikely. Tell her that I work for the *Bugle* and am trying to get some background information on the cast. There's an empty seat right next to me."

A couple of minutes later, Miles returned with the young woman in tow. Her large eyes glinted with interest and she offered a slim hand with bitten-off nails to Myrtle. "You're really amazing! Being a reporter at your age. That's so cool."

Myrtle shook her hand and gave her a tight smile. The girl was trying to be complimentary. There was no way for her to know that Myrtle preferred to be judged on her non-age-related accomplishments. Of which, in Myrtle's mind, there were many.

"Thank you my dear," she said graciously instead. "I'm Myrtle Clover."

The girl nodded absently. She seemed to totally miss the social prompt to introduce herself. Instead she was looking at the feet barely visible underneath the curtain. "I was supposed to be back there too," she said rather wistfully, as if she'd been left off a party invitation instead of not being part of a tragic death.

Miles said, "You're part of the cast?"

Of course she wasn't, since she wasn't backstage. She shook her head. "Not a speaking part, although I'm part of the ensemble at the very end. I wanted a speaking part, but I didn't make the cut in the audition. They didn't think I was exactly right. So instead, I help with sets and programs and stuff like that."

Myrtle couldn't see the girl playing the sultry role of Nandina. And Veronica was playing the part of an older woman. There didn't seem to be a good part for someone who looked this young and fresh-faced.

"But my car broke down on the way here tonight. I had to flag someone down for help."

Miles said disapprovingly, "Surely that's not a very safe thing to do. Even in a town like Bradley."

She pouted. "I was careful enough. Anyway, I ended up late. Thought I'd catch a couple of minutes of the play from the back of the theater before I slipped backstage. But, well, that's when they found Nandina."

"So you didn't actually see anything. That is, you don't have any information about the incident," said Myrtle.

The girl, whoever she was, was obviously the type who liked *knowing* things. She didn't want to let the opportunity pass to display some of this knowledge.

"Oh, I *know* things. I just don't know anything about what happened to Nandina. Although I have my suspicions." The girl arched her eyebrows.

"What are your suspicions? And, really, you need to give me your name. I don't like working with sources and not have any idea what their names are," said Myrtle. She fumbled in her large purse until she found a small notepad and a pencil. She poised the pencil expectantly.

"I'm Cady Flosser," said the girl. She spelled it. "I work a shift at Bo's Diner and I volunteer here and act here. Basically, I spend a lot of time with the cast. And I can tell you one thing—Nandina Marshall was trouble. I'm not at all surprised that someone ended up doing her in."

There was a note of vicious satisfaction in Cady's voice. Myrtle asked smoothly, "Were you also on the outs with Nandina?"

"Only some of the time. That's mainly because she liked playing the star. I tried out for her part in this play and I didn't get it. Nandina rubbed my face in it from that point on. But I didn't kill her. I must have still been getting out of the car when it happened."

Miles cleared his throat and pointed out, "You're using the word *kill*. You believe this to be murder, then?"

Cady blinked, her fake eyelashes fluttering as she did. "Well, of course I believe it to be murder. Nandina was totally healthy. And everyone hated her. But I don't *know* that it's murder, since I wasn't here. Look, if you want to talk to the cast for your story, you should come back here during rehearsals tomorrow. If we *have* rehearsals tomorrow." She watched as Red's deputy rolled out crime scene tape.

"Are rehearsals at night, then?" asked Myrtle.

"Suppertime. That's so cast members can work their day job, if they have one. Some do, some don't," said Cady. "If you want to talk to people before that, though, you probably can. Blaine, for instance. I already know where he'll be tomorrow morning. He'll be at the gym. He's there *every* morning at nine. He's a real structured guy."

Miles snorted and covered it up with a cough. Myrtle ignored him. Miles knew that Myrtle had an aversion to gyms, in general. But this aversion could be overcome in pursuit of justice.

Myrtle could tell by Cady's tone that she might have something of a crush on Blaine. She suspected that Cady, besides being something of a know-it-all, was a bit self-centered. So she tried flattery. "Thanks. I think it will be really helpful to talk to the cast members. But I'm also really interested in hearing *your* opinion on the cast. Just to give me a sort of overview."

Cady's eyes glinted. "I do know a lot about them. I'm really good at forming impressions of people, too. Like Blaine. You can tell he's such a hard worker. He's kind of a perfectionist so he'll come to rehearsal knowing all his lines *perfectly*. He's not just a good actor, either, because he's always writing and wants to be a playwright. And not just a *local* playwright, maybe someone who writes Broadway plays and things."

Miles, sitting behind Cady, made a face at Myrtle. As Myrtle had thought, Cady did seem to have a bad case of Blaine hero worship. She felt it might be more useful to move off the topic of Blaine altogether.

"What about that sort of dark man?" asked Myrtle quickly.

"Dark man?" asked Cady, mouthing the words as if they were unfamiliar to her.

Miles nodded. "You mean the real scruffy one. With the five o'clock shadow."

"It's not a five o'clock shadow. It's just a light beard for effect," said Myrtle.

"The effect is one that makes him appear he needs shaving," said Miles under his breath.

Cady said, "Oh, you're talking about Roscoe. You know how I mentioned that some of the cast has a day job and some don't? Well, he's one of the ones who doesn't. His wife is super-rich and Roscoe doesn't have to do anything but theater."

Miles's face too clearly demonstrated what he thought of this. "He doesn't *work*? It's not that he can't *find* a job, he just chooses not to have one?"

"I think he sometimes does some freelance accounting or something. But yeah—he doesn't have to work at all," said Cady with a shrug. "Although I really doubt he killed Nandina."

"Why is that?" asked Myrtle sharply.

Cady suddenly frowned, glancing toward the stage. "Sorry, got to run. The cops want to speak to me."

Myrtle turned to see Red motioning toward Cady. He gave his mother a reproving look and she gave him an innocent smile in return.

"So that's that," said Miles. "Looks like Red is going to shut down our little investigation."

"As if he could," said Myrtle smoothly. "We'll simply have to do our investigating when he's not around. I'm hoping, since Nandina was so unpopular, that the cast members will be happy to gossip about her."

Miles gestured to the stairs leading up to the stage. "There's one person who may have liked Nandina."

Myrtle turned to see the tall, awkward man wearing black framed glasses that she'd seen in the diner. He was crying in earnest.

CHAPTER FOUR

UNFORTUNATELY, THEIR time at the theater was a long one and they weren't able to talk to any other cast members or crew. Red had asked a few questions of them both—in particular about the "squabbling like children" remark that Myrtle had made to him earlier.

Despite the evening's unsettling events, Myrtle was surprised to discover she could fall asleep that night. But she couldn't *stay* asleep. Her rest ended abruptly at three-forty-five in the morning. She lay in the bed for a few minutes to see if rolling over would do or if she could think of nothing at all and drift off. As usual, any attempts to fall back asleep were completely useless. She got up, showered, dressed, and headed into her kitchen for an early breakfast.

It was about four-thirty when she heard a knock at her front door. She knew it had to be Miles. They were both chronic insomniacs and they frequently walked to each other's houses for coffee and breakfasts in the middle of the night. Still, she prudently peered out the side window in case it was Red. If Red were out there, she'd get a lecture about how she didn't look out the window before opening the door.

Miles was standing over to the far side of the door and looking apprehensively at the ground. Myrtle opened the door.

Miles gestured at the porch floor. "Pasha wants in," he said, giving the black cat a sideways look.

"What a darling! Pasha wants her mommy to give her breakfast?" crooned Myrtle. The feral cat brushed lovingly against Myrtle while giving Miles warning looks through narrowed eyes. Pasha had nothing to worry about—Miles was extremely wary of her, although he and the cat had developed something of an understanding recently.

"I'm not surprised you woke up early," said Myrtle over her shoulder as she thumped with her cane back to the kitchen.

"Woke up early?" said Miles. "I didn't sleep."

"Not at all?" Myrtle turned to study him. He did have bluish-purple circles under his eyes and his face was a bit drawn. "*That's* unusual for you. Usually you get *some* sleep. Either at the front end of the night or the back end."

"I suppose it was due to the evening's events," said Miles. Myrtle opened a can of cat food for Pasha and Miles took over Myrtle's scrambled egg making. After botching cracking two eggs in a row, however, Myrtle shooed him away.

"You're clearly too exhausted to do anything. You'll have to be the silent sidekick today or who knows what you might say." Myrtle started whisking the eggs as Miles searched in her cabinet for the largest coffee-holding container he could find.

"This should work," he muttered.

Myrtle glanced at the object in his hand. "That's technically a soup bowl. But who cares? It'll probably do you good to fill it up and drink it."

"What's on the agenda for this morning?" asked Miles as he poured himself a tremendous cup of coffee. Upon noticing that he'd wiped out the entire pot, he set about making more.

"We're going to the gym to see Blaine," said Myrtle. "Cady said that was his normal morning routine."

Miles winced. "Not the gym. I'm not sure I'll be able to exercise."

"There's a group of old men there who just sit in the lobby and drink coffee," said Myrtle. "I never see them exercise."

"Not that you exercise yourself very often," pointed out Miles.

"I do on occasion. Particularly when there is a murder suspect exercising. We've had a few cases now where our suspects have liked to exercise. Or worked at the gym," said Myrtle thoughtfully as she stirred the eggs.

"I wish we'd have more suspects that enjoyed sitting on sofas," said Miles. Having made another pot of coffee, he was now turning his attention to his own cup. He put a quarter cup of sugar into the bowl of coffee and stirred it carefully, tapping the spoon on the side to keep it from dripping when he was done.

"By the way, did you talk to Wanda about my plan to get her a column with the *Bugle*?" asked Myrtle.

"I did indeed. She was delighted."

Myrtle said, "Then I suppose I should try to fit in a trip to the newspaper office with Wanda to introduce her to Sloan."

Miles smiled. "I'd like to see that."

"You will. I don't have a car, remember?"

Miles sighed. "Right. Or maybe I can lend you mine. Let me see how much energy I have left later in the day."

"I suppose you should go back home after your coffee and change into exercise-related gear," said Myrtle. She glanced at his khaki pants and button-down shirt.

"Not if I'm only sitting in the lobby with the old guys," said Miles. He took an experimental sip of the coffee and immediately added more sugar.

Myrtle was looking in her fridge with great concentration. "I could have sworn that I got bacon at the store with Red. Where on earth is it?"

"Did you stock up?" asked Miles. "Things were looking pretty bare here yesterday."

"I stocked up, but I'd neglected to make a list before Red arrived. He's rather critical of any lapses on my part, so I pretended my list was in my head."

Miles snorted. "How did *that* work out for you?"

"Apparently not very well if I ended up without bacon." Myrtle sighed. "I just picked up whatever was on sale. Now I'm not sure exactly what meals I can make with this stuff. I'll likely have to have Elaine take me back to the store."

Miles's nose wrinkled. "Myrtle, those eggs are starting to get rather malodorous."

Myrtle exclaimed sharply and turned back to the stove. She used a metal spatula on the eggs and found that the eggs were reluctant to be moved from the bottom of the pan.

"Shoot. Eggs are such delicate things," she fussed. She gave Miles a suspicious sideways glance to ensure he wasn't looking smug about her cooking snafu.

Miles decided to silently sip his coffee.

"Here, they're just fried on one side and scrambled on the other," said Myrtle. She used a bit of muscle to scrape the eggs from the bottom of the pan and slide them onto a plate. She shoved the plate in front of Miles. He stared at it.

"Think of it as innovation in the kitchen," said Myrtle. She fixed herself a plate, too, and put a good deal of cheese on the top. Miles reached a hand out for the bag of shredded cheese after she was done.

"Are you actually planning on exercising, Myrtle?" asked Miles dubiously. He looked over at his passenger. She had on a pair of khaki pants with an elastic waistband that she appeared to fondly consider exercise gear. The pants were accompanied by a diaphanous white crew neck top that could have doubled as a basic dressy top if it had been paired with black pants. The bottom line was that she didn't appear to be ready for a rigorous workout.

"If it becomes necessary, I will. Although I'm strongly hoping that it doesn't become necessary. I'd like to catch Blaine either coming into the gym or leaving it," said Myrtle.

"Might lurking become necessary?" asked Miles. He tried fighting back a slight smile.

"It might. The trick is to look as if I'm *willing* to exercise without actually exercising." They pulled up into the gym parking lot and Myrtle exclaimed, "What in heaven's name are all these people doing here?"

"Exercising. Allegedly. Unless they're all lurking," said Miles, pulling into a spot. "Or drinking coffee with the old guys in the lobby as I'll be doing."

"Must they all be exercising when we're trying to investigate a murder?" Myrtle sighed. "I hope we can find Blaine in the sweaty hordes. It's so very *early* to be exercising, isn't it?"

"I suppose," said Miles, struggling against the small smile again, "that these people work."

"Hmm." Myrtle had worked for decades as a schoolteacher. But her longevity meant that she'd received retirement pay for longer than she'd ever taught. Work was fast becoming a dim memory.

It was just as busy inside the gym. "This is almost as bad as the diner yesterday," said Myrtle.

Miles scanned the lobby. "He doesn't seem to be out here, Myrtle. He must be in one of the exercise rooms."

"Pooh." Myrtle made a face. "What if I'm trying to walk on the treadmill and I miss Blaine as he heads out?"

"If you do miss him, then I'll catch him on my end. Then I can text your phone to let you know that I've waylaid him," suggested Miles.

Myrtle beamed at him. "How very helpful of you, Miles! That sounds like an excellent idea." She hesitated. "You're sure you won't get too involved with the old fellows and the coffee to remember your part?"

"That's unlikely," said Miles dryly. "The conversations I have with them are never sparkling. They're also the same fellows who frequently hang out in front of the gas station."

"And on the bench in front of the diner, don't they?" asked Myrtle, crinkling her brow.

"That's a different set of old boys. Most of the time, anyway."

"Really? They look the same. All wearing baseball hats and plaid shirts. All right, I'm heading back there." Myrtle squared her shoulders, firmly grasped her cane, and strode purposefully back to a large, fully-mirrored, brightly-lit exercise room. The things she did in the line of duty during an investigation astonished her.

The exercise room itself was always overwhelming. Not only did the mirrors create a very odd illusion, but there was so much external stimulation. There was high-energy music being pumped out of the intercom, the sound of weights and people running on treadmills, and a constant hum from the various workout machines in the room. Resolutely, Myrtle headed for an open treadmill, scanning for Blaine as she did.

She was nearly overcome with relief when she spotted Blaine finishing up with free weights at the end of the room. He appeared to be heading her way, meaning that she wouldn't have to even go through the pretense of walking on the treadmill. But then he stopped by the weight machines, pausing to wait his turn while someone else exercised.

Myrtle brightened. She could ask him to show her how to work a weight machine. Even though she knew very well how to, she just chose to avoid them if at all possible.

Myrtle grasped her cane and hurried over to Blaine. Looking as frail as a woman standing at six feet could possibly appear, she said, "Do you know how to work these machines?"

He turned to her and his grin lit up his entire face. His eyes twinkled, a dimple appeared and disappeared, and his teeth shone white against his lightly tanned skin. "I sure do. May I have the honor of showing you how to use them?" He gave a small bow and grinned up at her.

Myrtle recognized this type of flirtatious deference. It was a trait very endearing to most elderly ladies. She was not most elderly ladies. But, for this situation a flustered laugh and thrilled acceptance was required, which she easily managed. Perhaps she should go on the stage herself.

"That would be simply grand. Thank you, my dear. Just this one. Just this machine here." Myrtle pointed to a weight machine that focused on arms. Even a complete idiot would know how to use it—one only had to sit in the seat, put one's hands into the loops, set the weights to the correct level, and then pull up. But playing the role of a complete idiot worked well for Myrtle. It meant that she might be able to trick Blaine into revealing more information than he'd planned on.

Blaine gallantly showed Myrtle how to work the weight machine while she watched, trying her best to appear raptly fascinated and ask related questions.

"Does that make sense?" Blaine asked solicitously at the end of his spiel.

"It certainly does. Thanks so much. Now I can strengthen my core a bit. I've heard that's so important as we get older." Myrtle then switched gears quickly. She tilted her head quizzically to one side. "You know, you look awfully familiar." She snapped her fingers. "I know. You were in that play, weren't you?"

A shadow passed briefly across Blaine's handsome features. Then he nodded. "That's right."

He looked across the room at the door, clearly wanting to escape. Myrtle said quickly, "Are you originally from here?"

He relaxed a little, giving her that dazzling white smile again. "No, I only moved here a few years ago. The lake is really what brought me to Bradley. I love writing my poetry and looking out on the lake." There was a self-deprecating tone to his voice as he talked about his poetry.

Myrtle said, "I'm sure spending time at the lake must be very relaxing. And I'd imagine that relaxation is definitely in order right now."

He gave a confused frown and Myrtle continued, "Because of that terrible incident last night. I was in the audience, you see. The poor girl. Nandina, wasn't that her name? What a lovely young woman."

Blaine winced as if her name caused him pain. He slowly said, "Yes, Nandina. It's a horrible tragedy." He looked longingly at the door again.

"The police didn't find out what happened? Or who was responsible?" asked Myrtle in a hushed, gossipy voice.

Blaine cleared his throat. "They seemed to believe it was foul play."

"Did they?" Myrtle asked with carefully modulated horrified surprise.

"I'm afraid so. She was ... strangled." Blaine swallowed hard and put a hand to his own throat as if in sympathy.

This, at least, was new information. The poor girl. On a stage, with so many people around?

She hadn't realized she'd said the last bit out loud until Blaine answered her. "It's bizarre, isn't it? But you see, the cast was coming and going and the lights were dimmed. It was a set change. So there was opportunity. And the set change music was playing, of course."

And that would have obscured any odd noises. The set change music was quite loud. She and Miles had made faces at each other at the time.

"Barbaric!" said Myrtle. "And for such a thing to happen at our little community theater!"

Blaine sighed. "I know. I hope having a violent crime there won't drive people away. Poor Mr. Toucan."

"Oh, on the contrary," said Myrtle sharply. "It will bring them there in droves. People are so ghoulish." She put on her Worried Old Lady face. "Do you have any idea who might be responsible for the poor girl's death?"

"I don't have the foggiest idea. Nandina could sometimes be difficult to work with, but *murder*?" His voice trailed off.

"Surely there must have been *someone* who seems as if they could be responsible," said Myrtle in a wheedling tone.

"I don't know," he repeated, although Myrtle thought he might be thinking of something. He hesitated and then said, "I will say that Skip Rogers is sort of an odd guy. But I can't imagine he would do something like this," he added hurriedly. "And he acted like he was crazy about Nandina."

Myrtle tried to remember the photos and names from the program she'd studied that morning. "Skip. Is he that sort of morose young man with glasses? Tall and thin?"

Blaine was nodding before she'd even finished her description. It also matched the description of the man she'd seen weeping at the theater.

Blaine now did appear to be done and Myrtle decided not to make him guarded by asking more questions. He'd find out soon enough that she worked for the newspaper. For now, she had at least found out information without having to push Red for details. She glanced at her watch. "Oh my, is that the time? I should go."

Blaine drew his eyebrows together in a frown. "Weren't you going to exercise? Use the weight machine?"

"Yes. But all this talk of murder is rather draining. I think that's enough for today. Now I know how to use the machine for the next time I come in." Which will likely be a year or more from now, decided Myrtle with a small shudder.

When Myrtle entered the lobby she saw with a smile that Miles appeared bored and sleepy. The old boys must not be very entertaining today.

"Ready to head out?" she asked.

He leaped to his feet with alacrity. "Yes. Yes, I think it's time." He turned to his companions who were still speaking to each other in desultory tones. "See you fellows later." He left with Myrtle, appearing greatly relieved.

"What was their focus of conversation today?" asked Myrtle dryly as they walked out of the gym.

"Unfortunately, Bud appeared to have some sort of issue with his kidney," said Miles. "His in-depth narrative seemed to spur the others to chime in with their own specific health issues, which all tended to revolve around their digestive systems."

Myrtle made a face. "I'm glad I was spared all of that. I get enough digestive system banter when I'm trapped in conversations with my neighbor."

"Erma is simply trying to connect," said Miles. He struggled with a smile as he unlocked his car.

Myrtle gave him a withering look.

"All right, talking about Erma clearly isn't going to improve your mood. Tell me what happened with Blaine," said Miles.

"He's a very self-aware young man," said Myrtle thoughtfully as she got into the car. "I think he's very used to people *liking* him. He knows how to turn on the charm, even with octogenarians. And he was reluctant to speak ill of the other suspects."

"So you didn't really get anything out of him?" asked Miles as he backed up the car.

"He did agree that Nandina was hard to work with. She clearly wasn't a Sunday school teacher, although we knew that from the little we overheard at the diner yesterday. And he said something about Skip Rogers being strange, although he immediately qualified the statement, saying that he couldn't imagine him murdering anyone."

Miles said, "Which one is Skip again? I need to study that program."

"He's the one we saw tearing up last night at the theater. The tall, awkward one in the glasses."

Miles said, "Oh, that's right. He was the only one defending Nandina at the diner, as I recall. I wonder what he saw in Nandina that no one else did."

Myrtle snorted. "I don't think it was some sort of soulful quality that Nandina possessed. I suspect it had more to do with the girl's looks. He clearly had a crush on her."

"So that should eliminate him from the list of suspects," said Miles.

"I don't think so. What if Skip had convinced himself that he was in love with Nandina and then she fell for someone else? He might have felt crushed and betrayed enough to murder Nandina. Strangulation is a very personal crime, after all."

Miles took one of his hands off the wheel and pulled uncomfortably at his shirt collar. "Strangulation? Is that how she died?"

"That was something else I learned from Blaine—the method by which she was killed. Which was good to find out, since otherwise, I'd have had to bug Red to uncover that tidbit and he would try to shut down my investigating," said Myrtle darkly.

"Okay. So Skip could have felt betrayed by Nandina and murdered her in frustration," said Miles. "But would he be so upset afterward? If he were responsible?"

"Sure. Because he *loved* her. He'd mourn her death even if he *were* responsible," said Myrtle. "Simply because she's not around anymore."

"Very dark and psychological," muttered Miles as he pulled the car onto their street. He squinted. "Oh no. Who is that in my driveway?"

It was a rusted-out ancient Pontiac with cardboard duct taped over a missing window.

"I'm no psychic, but I suspect that's Wanda," said Myrtle. "Her brother must have taken one of the cars off the cinder blocks, stuck some tires on, and repaired it enough to make it usable."

"Oh goody," muttered Miles.

"Don't drop me off yet," said Myrtle. "I want to hear what Wanda has to say. Besides, this saves me a trip. I was going to have to go pick her up to take her to the newspaper office."

"Is she sitting in her car?" asked Miles, sounding anxious as he pulled the Volvo into his driveway. "Why don't I see her?"

A straggly figure with a leathery face opened Miles's front door, briefly waved with a bony hand, then closed the door again.

"How did she get inside?" Miles turned off the engine.

"Did you leave your door unlocked? One should never leave one's door unlocked, even in a small town." Myrtle gave him a reproachful look. "Red always says that it's really just as wicked to tempt someone as it is to do the stealing."

"Since when did you start quoting Red?" asked Miles hotly. "And that's the most ridiculous thing I've ever heard. It certainly is *not* as wicked as stealing. Besides, I don't leave my door unlocked, *ever*. I'm from Atlanta, remember? I'm not exactly a trusting soul. Which is why I'm not thrilled to find Wanda roaming around my house."

Myrtle was already halfway up Miles's walk, thumping her cane on the cement robustly. "Let's hear what she has to say."

CHAPTER FIVE

MYRTLE WAS FIRST THROUGH Miles's door. "Wanda! How are you? Everything going well?"

Wanda was sitting primly on Miles's sofa as if she were a guest for the queen. A large paper bag sat at her feet. "Everything is good. Better than it is for you, anyway. Because yer in danger."

Myrtle nodded absently. "Oh, don't I know it! I'm always in danger, though. You should really start predicting when I'm *not* in danger, Wanda. It might make it more of a challenge for you."

Miles finally made it through the door. "Wanda, what on earth are you doing here? And how did you get in?"

Wanda shrugged an emaciated shoulder. "With yer hide-a-key."

Miles stared at her. "But that's in a secret location!"

Myrtle grinned at him. "Do you keep it under your mat?"

"Certainly not!"

Wanda said, "He keeps it taped to the bottom of his sprinkler in the bushes."

Miles opened his mouth and closed it.

Myrtle said, "She *is* a psychic, Miles. For heaven's sake."

"It's hot out there," said Wanda with another shrug. "Wanted a bit of air."

Miles just kept staring.

Myrtle ignored him and said eagerly to Wanda, "What can we do for you today? You didn't just come here to warn me, did you?"

"No. But you do need to watch your step. Some of them actors have evil in their hearts," intoned Wanda, her dark eyes serious.

Myrtle and Miles stared wordlessly at her.

Then Wanda gave a rattling, nicotine infested laugh. "And I brought y'all squash. Been growing it. Keeps coming in. I want to give it to Miles. He's been nice to me. Both of y'all have—the job and everything."

Miles quickly covered up his horrified response. "Thanks, Wanda."

Myrtle thought she remembered that Miles had a massive aversion to squash. This should be interesting. Her bag seemed to be loaded down with them.

"You drove here? Dan got one of the cars working?" asked Myrtle.

A look of pride crossed Wanda's features. "Sure did. Yanked it right off them cement blocks with some help from the boys down the street. Slapped some tires on it, stuck some kind of wire under the hood and off it went. Wished he had thunk to do it yesterday when I walked here."

"That's really wonderful. Wonderful. And I hope Crazy Dan knew what he was doing and you get home safely. Although first, I do want us to go into town and talk to my editor, Sloan. I suppose he's your editor now, too. And, while you're here, Wanda, do you have any insights at all into the theater murder?"

"What, that young girl?" grated Wanda.

"That's right."

Miles was still staring at the huge bag of squash.

Wanda said laconically, "Not really."

Myrtle persisted. "But you said that some actors have evil in their hearts! Were you being gender specific and meaning *male actors*? Or were you being politically correct and meaning male *or female* actors."

Finally there was a reaction from Miles. He gave a sputtering chuckle at Myrtle using "politically correct" in relation to Wanda.

"I'm saying it's a right mess," said Wanda darkly. "And to watch yer step."

"Okay. Message received." Myrtle looked at her watch. "Let's walk down and see Sloan at the *Bugle*. Sometimes he leaves to interview people for stories. And sometimes to eat or belly up to a nearby bar. It'll only take a minute. I just need to let him know that his worries about the horoscope are over."

Miles muttered, "And put him on the spot so that he can't turn you down."

"Whatever works," said Myrtle.

"I kin drive us," said Wanda. "That way you don't have to walk none."

"It's not far," said Myrtle.

"Yeah, but I kinda got a hankerin' to drive. Ain't done much of it for a while," said Wanda.

Miles asked, "Are we sure we wouldn't like to offer Sloan a little squash too?" in a hopeful voice.

"Them's fer you," said Wanda more forcefully than she usually spoke.

The old Pontiac Catalina leered at them with its large, rusted grill and wide, round headlights. Myrtle yanked on the passenger door handle and then carefully slid onto the vinyl seat with scattered cigarette burns. Myrtle looked at the chrome window crank and the radio dials and the thin, fake wood steering wheel. "I feel as if I've traveled back in time to the late 1960s," she said.

"Enjoy yer ride," said Wanda with a grin. "This thang has horsepower. Plus power steering an' power brakes."

She wasn't kidding about the horsepower. Wanda pressed on the accelerator and the vehicle shot forward with an excited roar. Myrtle clung to the door for dear life.

They were in downtown Bradley in a matter of seconds. "That it there?" asked Wanda, pointing.

"Right there. And there's a parking place directly in front," said Myrtle.

Even luckier than the parking spot was the fact that Sloan was actually trying to do some work in the newsroom. She and Wanda entered the newsroom from the sunny outside and took a second to let their eyes adjust to the dim light inside. Myrtle thought once again that Sloan would do well to open a couple of windows and let sunshine and fresh air dispel some of the gloom and mustiness. As usual, there were stacks and stacks of papers on every surface, including the floor. Wanda seemed unconcerned about the clutter—it was just like home.

Sloan was always uneasy with Myrtle. He had been a former student of hers and she did not consider him one of her greater successes, despite the fact that he ended up being editor, and even publisher, of the *Bradley Bugle* newspaper. One of Myrtle's favorite pastimes was to correct the newspaper in red ink and mail it over to the newsroom. Plus, there was the fact that Sloan was really a lackey for Red and had brought Myrtle on to keep her busy and out of trouble. When Sloan spotted Myrtle, he rose hastily from his seat, an anxious look on his broad face. "Miss Myrtle!" He always sounded as if he'd been caught in the middle of making spitballs or pulling someone's ponytail.

Myrtle made an effort to be especially kind and gentle since she needed to get Wanda employed. She said, "Good morning, Sloan! How are things going here?"

"Oh fine, fine. Just trying to write up a few things for the next edition." He smiled at her, although his eyes were a bit quizzical as he looked at Wanda. No wonder. Wanda was stick-thin with straggly hair that she'd attempted to pull back into a plastic clasp. She had that jittery look about her that meant a cigarette wasn't far in her future. Her skin was as yellow as her nicotine-stained fingers and when she grinned at Sloan, there were not many teeth on display.

"Good to see you this morning, Sloan. I wanted to introduce you to the best thing to happen to the *Bradley Bugle*."

Sloan gave Wanda a dubious smile.

"This is Wanda ... well ... just Wanda." Myrtle didn't want to admit that, *if* she'd ever caught Wanda's last name, she'd forgotten it along the way. "I think, actually, we'll go with sort of a show name for Wanda. Madam Wanda. Or Wanda the Magnificent." Wanda's last name finally came to her and she smiled with relief. "Alewine. Yes, or we could go with a regular byline of Wanda Alewine."

"Wanda the Magnificent sounds more like a magician," noted Wanda laconically.

Sloan was now looking even more anxious. "I'm sorry, but I don't know what you're talking about. Is Wanda a ... journalist?"

"Naw!" said Wanda with feeling.

Myrtle said, "No, Wanda is a gifted seer. She can tell things that will happen in the future."

"Is that so?" asked Sloan. He started rubbing his large forehead as he frequently did when agitated.

"Since you don't have a resident writer for our popular horoscope column, I have procured one for you. The difference is that Wanda has talent. She won't be simply making things up, she'll be giving fortunes," explained Myrtle.

Sloan looked conflicted. "Well, it's true that we've had a hard time keeping horoscope writers around. There was poor Willow, for example."

"Always warning about steering clear of skinny Scorpio men," clucked Myrtle.

"Before her there was Maisy. And Maisy had her nerves, you know."

Myrtle rolled her eyes. "Because horoscope manufacturing is so *brutal*. The way it's done for the Bradley paper is less dabbling in the dark arts and more to do with looking at pretty stars and inventing story lines. That's why we need Wanda. Wanda is *real*." And desperately needs money or else Miles would lose all of his through selflessness. And then Myrtle would have no one to do things around town with.

Sloan politely addressed Wanda, "Do you have a portfolio? Any writing samples I can take a look at?"

Wanda gave Myrtle a sideways look.

"She doesn't," admitted Myrtle. "That's because she's something of a find. You know how those artsy people found those incredible folk artists in these really depressed Southern rural towns? Wanda is like that."

"Wanda does art?" Sloan was looking confused again.

"No, Wanda is just *special*. A diamond in the rough," said Myrtle. "And I personally will ensure that I edit out any roughness this particular diamond produces."

Sloan brightened. "I see. Excellent. All right then." He extended a hand to Wanda. "Most excellent to meet you, uh, Wanda the Wonderful?" He glanced over at Myrtle. "A bit of alliteration there. I haven't forgotten *everything* you taught me in school."

Myrtle bit her tongue and beamed beneficently at him.

Wanda smiled back at him. She had clearly decided to leave the talking up to Myrtle. But as they turned to go, Wanda did make one statement. "Call the plumber."

Sloan's smile grew so tight that it looked as though it might break.

"It's probably a good idea," said Myrtle with a shrug.

Myrtle decided not to mention the fact that she was going to write an investigative report on Nandina's murder. Perhaps she shouldn't press things during *this* visit. Sloan was starting to look stressed out.

Wanda dropped Myrtle back home and said, "I'll brang horoscopes for you tomorrow. You'll make 'em look good?"

"They'll look great, I promise," said Myrtle. "See you tomorrow."

Miles had apparently been waiting for Myrtle to arrive back home. When Myrtle answered the door, he stood there holding the brown bag that Wanda had brought. "Whatever am I going to do with this squash?"

"Don't be a baby. We'll make something with it," said Myrtle. She did eye the bag uneasily, however. Squash wasn't her most favorite vegetable either.

"Make something? Not something to *eat*, I hope. Because I won't," said Miles with more conviction than Myrtle had heard in his voice for a while.

"Of course something to eat! One doesn't exactly make *bridges* out of squash, you know. If you insist on saying you were an engineer, you should know that. I believe I will make a squash casserole. Maybe that will even win us some sympathy with the cast if we present it to them as a sympathy gift," said Myrtle, staring thoughtfully at the bulging bag.

Miles muttered, "Not if *you're* making it."

"What was that?" asked Myrtle.

"Nothing." Miles sighed. "I guess a casserole—a very large casserole—is the only way of getting rid of the squash. I just have a feeling that our squash casserole will end up being given away from recipient to recipient, much like a fruit cake. You might want to bake it in a disposable container."

"Nonsense. If I bake it in a glass dish, then I have the perfect excuse for going back for another talk with our suspects. Because I have to collect the dish, you see. It's the very best way," said Myrtle.

She walked into her kitchen and pulled a couple of old cookbooks off the shelf. Miles trailed along behind her. He sat at her kitchen table and she pushed a cookbook in front of him. "Here. You look through this one for a good squash casserole and I'll check this one. I'll whip it up real quick and then we can bake it. While it bakes, we can pop across the street and talk to Elaine. See if she has any insights into the cast members, since she volunteers over there."

Miles said uneasily, "I don't know if I want any responsibility for the casserole. I mean, seeing as it's your idea and everything."

"Don't be silly—it's your squash, after all."

Miles made a face. "Those are two words that shouldn't go with each other. *Your squash*." He paused. "I thought you still had very odd ingredients in the house. Because of your grocery shopping trip with Red."

"I do. But I should certainly have something to make squash casserole with." She peered closer at a yellowed cookbook in front of her. "Here's one. Looks pretty basic."

"Good," muttered Miles.

"Check and see if I have sour cream and shredded cheese," instructed Myrtle as she got up to pull out a glass casserole dish.

She carefully sprayed the bottom of it with cooking spray as Miles investigated the contents of her refrigerator.

"I don't see any sour cream," reported Miles from the depths of the fridge. "But somehow you have two open mayonnaises. And barbeque sauce."

"I suppose they were on sale. What about cheese?" asked Myrtle.

"No shredded cheese. But you do have feta cheese. Oddly."

"There's nothing odd about feta, Miles. I suppose it must have been on sale, too. Well, we'll have to make do, won't we? Cooking is all about being creative."

Miles retreated from the refrigerator with the feta and the mayo and his face said that he wasn't so sure. "I thought cooking was all about knowing the rules first before you break them."

"Oh nooo, Miles. That's such a limited view of the culinary arts. Amazing recipes are created by using our imaginations!"

Miles looked glum as he sat down again.

"Here. Slice up the squash while you're sitting." Myrtle pushed a large amount of squash in front of Miles and he eyed it with misgiving.

"How should I slice it?" he asked.

"I think in large pieces. Right? I do hate it when I'm eating casseroles and I can't tell what the ingredients are because they're shredded to bits. No, this will be a hearty casserole. A casserole to breathe life back into the mourning cast at the theater!" Myrtle brandished a knife dramatically.

Miles said, "I hope it'll breathe life into them instead of the other way around. What are you doing with that knife?"

"I have to cut the onion up for the casserole and sauté it," said Myrtle.

"I didn't see any onion in the fridge," Miles pointed out. "And I don't see it on the counter, either."

Myrtle frowned. "I could have sworn I had some onion. No worries. I'll pull something out of the spice rack."

Miles rubbed his forehead as if it were hurting him. "I hope it's minced onion. Or perhaps powdered onion."

"Onion salt!" said Myrtle triumphantly as various spices fell out of her cabinet. "Perfect!" She glanced over at Miles, who was half-heartedly pushing the knife into the squash. "For heaven's sake. It won't bite you. A little more *vigor* please, Miles! Elbow grease!"

A few minutes later, he said, "This is all sliced up. It's ready for the skillet, I think."

Myrtle was mixing together what looked like an entire jar of mayonnaise with the feta cheese. "What skillet?"

Miles said, "I believe it's customary to pre-cook squash before it goes into the casserole dish."

"Why on earth would we do that? We've already got the oven pre-heated. The *oven* will cook it."

"I'm only saying that it's customary. It's quite a lot of squash, you know. In very *chunky* pieces. Perhaps you should check your recipe to make sure," said Miles. He took a paper towel and carefully removed any remnants of squash from his fingers.

"But you know, I've never really cared for the Southern style of vegetable. The kind that is overcooked that it falls apart. They're just cooked to death, aren't they?"

Miles said, "That's practically sacrilegious from a Southern-er."

"Still, it's the truth. I'm sure Southern cooks are zapping all the vitamins and minerals out of the food by letting it cook on the stove half the day. Ours will be a *robust* squash casserole!" Myrtle mixed squash into the mayonnaise blend until it all but disappeared in the whiteness of it.

"Please leave me out as a co-cook. All I did was cut the vegetables to your specifications. And I'm not sure you should extol the healthy qualities of your casserole considering all the mayonnaise that composes it," said Miles. "Does the recipe require that much mayo?"

"Squash is so bland that you *need* a lot a mayonnaise. The mayo *makes* the casserole," said Myrtle with conviction as she slid it into the oven. "Now let's go see Elaine."

"Shouldn't we keep an eye on the casserole? Having an unwatched oven sounds like a recipe for disaster. Actually, the entire casserole seems like a recipe for disaster," said Miles.

Myrtle ignored his misgivings. "Don't be so fretful, Miles. We'll be directly across the street. I'll keep an eye on the time."

"I doubt Red would like the sound of this," said Miles uneasily.

"Which is exactly why we won't tell him."

Miles decided to pull out his cell phone and set a timer. The recipe had said thirty minutes.

As was frequently the case, it was fairly chaotic at Elaine and Red's house across the street. That was one hundred percent due to Jack Clover. Jack was nearly three years old and sometimes had more energy in his small body than fifty professional athletes put together. Today was one of the days where this energy was in evidence. Miles and Myrtle moved aside several plastic trucks to sit gingerly on the den sofa and watched as Jack ran around the room in circles, grinning as he went.

Elaine had retreated to get them some ice waters. Miles muttered, "I believe I'd have preferred something stronger. Do you think Jack has just consumed a bag of candy?"

"No, I believe he's being an airplane," said Myrtle, beaming at the toddler. "Clever boy."

"If he were being an airplane, wouldn't he have his arms out?" asked Miles, his eyes following Jack as he ran.

"A minor technicality," said Myrtle.

Jack chose that moment to stop running. He came up to Myrtle and rested his sweaty head on her knee. She rubbed his small back and he gave a contented sigh.

"See? Now he's ready for a nap," said Myrtle.

"*I'm* ready for a nap," said Miles.

"No naps!" said Elaine as she entered the den with a tray of waters. "Jack isn't taking morning naps anymore or else he won't take an afternoon one. And I *really* need him to take the afternoon one. Here, I'll turn on one of his shows and he can have a little quiet time while we talk."

The danger with turning on one of Jack's shows was that Myrtle and Miles would get pulled into it and completely distracted by the task at hand. The shows were frequently surreal and featured lively animation along with people in costumes dancing to catchy tunes. Myrtle told herself firmly that this time she would not be sucked in. She gave Miles a reproving look when she saw him watching a six-foot tall dog dance with a princess in an animated background that looked like it had come from a Van Gogh painting.

Elaine settled into a recliner and for a moment looked relaxed and sleepy enough to drift off. It must have been an early morning with Jack. She took a sip of her water and then asked, "I guess the play last night was more exciting than it was supposed to be, wasn't it?"

"It certainly was!" said Myrtle. "Did Red fill you in on it?"

Elaine made a face. "Not nearly as much as I'd have liked. He just sketched out the basics and then proceeded to ask me a lot of questions about the cast."

Miles looked sideways at Myrtle. It sounded very much like their plan now.

Myrtle said, "I don't know a lot more than you do, Elaine. But the death happened not far into the play. It was that scene where Nandina was sleeping on stage. Except she wasn't sleeping."

Elaine nodded thoughtfully. "Poor Nandina. But that does make sense, from a killer's point of view. It was during a set change so the lights would have been off, or at least really dim. I know the set change music was really loud and lively and would have covered up any strange sounds. Most of the cast would have been on stage helping to move the set around, which is what you get when you have a small production."

Miles dragged his eyes away from the TV and the large dog, which was now inexplicably playing hopscotch with an orange dinosaur. "What I don't understand is why she didn't fight back. We're not talking about a frail person here. Nandina was in the prime of her life and full of energy and determination. Why didn't she punch her attacker or scream or something like that?"

Elaine said, "She would have expected cast members to be near her, getting the set ready. These were people she *knew*, not some strangers. Besides, Red said that she'd been drinking. She *always* had a glass of wine before she went out on the stage. Or more. Everybody knew it. Not only that, but there was evidence of sleeping pills in her glass. Not enough to kill her, but enough to make her very, very sleepy. It's always crazy backstage before a show and it would have been super-easy to put something in her glass. And having the cast members around her during the set change wouldn't have been alarming at all."

"Her guard would have been down," said Myrtle nodding.

"Not only that, but what if, when the murder actually happened, she wasn't able to make a sound. You know? From ... the pressure," said Miles.

They all swallowed.

Myrtle said, "But I'm still not really straight on this, Elaine. Wouldn't the cast members be able to say who was close enough to Nandina to kill her? Couldn't they tell if someone wasn't doing their set-up job and was instead murdering a fellow cast member?"

Elaine said, "You'd think so. But really, it's a little chaotic, at least the time or two I've observed it when I've been volunteering at the theater. Everyone is rushing around, music is playing loudly for the audience during the set change, and everyone would probably be intent on what they were doing. Plus, the lighting back there was really dim so they may not have been able to see much. If someone were near Nandina's bed on the stage, it probably wouldn't have looked out of the ordinary—the bed was the most important set piece on the stage at that time."

"Who do you think might have wanted to get rid of Nandina?" asked Myrtle. "What kind of an impression did you get of Nandina and the other cast members?"

Elaine thought about this for a few seconds. "I think they all were hard workers. They were all passionate about the theater. Some of the actors might have been more mature than others, but they were all professional in terms of their acting. Nandina did think a lot of herself, though."

"Was that justified?" asked Myrtle.

"Well, she was certainly beautiful. And she had a great sense of style, which showcased her beauty. She was a good actress, but sometimes her attitude got in the way. Sometimes she made everyone really annoyed from acting smug or condescending or like she was doing them a favor by acting in a small production in a small town," said Elaine. "I can't think specifically who disliked her. Although Veronica comes to mind, since she was being treated like a has-been and Nandina was a starlet."

Miles said, "So Nandina thought she had a big future?"

"I suppose she did. Hollywood or New York or something. It's kind of sad," said Elaine.

Since Elaine didn't seem to have much else to say about the cast and since she was now looking somewhat deflated by their conversation (and perhaps from tiredness resulting from getting up before the sun with Jack), Myrtle changed direction and started chatting about Jack and Red and other things that were going on. Miles became absorbed again in the odd children's show, watching it almost as avidly as Jack was. At least, he was until his phone started making urgent beeping noises.

"What in heaven's name is that?" asked Myrtle in alarm.

"It's not one of those severe weather alerts, is it?" asked Elaine with concern. "I haven't had a chance to see the forecast today."

Jack was the only one who was unconcerned. He smiled faintly as the dinosaur dumped a bucket of water over the dog's head.

Miles fumbled with his phone. "It's this timer. Oops." He dropped his cell phone underneath the sofa.

"Here, I can get it," said Elaine over the persistent beeping.

That was the moment Red came in. "What is *that*?" he asked loudly.

Miles colored as Elaine handed him the phone. "It's just my phone."

"Why is it doing that, though?" asked Red with concern.

"It's a timer." Miles quickly turned the timer off, glancing meaningfully sideways at Myrtle. "Myrtle, we should probably go."

But Myrtle appeared to have completely forgotten about the squash casserole and she hadn't been aware that Miles was setting a timer to keep track of the time it had been in her oven.

Myrtle frowned at him. "But then I won't have a chance to chat with Red," she said pointedly.

"I know, but we really should be getting back," said Miles. "Remember? We have other things we need to do today."

Red said, "And my lips are sealed, Mama, if you're wanting to talk with me about the case. Completely sealed." He completely ruined the effect of this statement by opening his mouth to take a bite of an apple he'd grabbed on the way into the house.

"I just have one minor question for you, Red, that's all," said Myrtle. "I met this charming little girl last night at the theater. She was telling me this story about car trouble and I kept hoping she wasn't just spinning a yarn. Very likeable girl."

Red nodded. "Ahhh ... Cady."

"That's right. Did you check her alibi yet? I just hate to think she could have been involved when she was so nice," said Myrtle.

Red's eyes narrowed a bit as if he had a feeling that she wasn't interested solely because the girl was pleasant. "I did, Mama. The girl is clear."

Myrtle decided to quit while she was ahead and moved on to other topics. Miles appeared increasingly agitated as another fifteen minutes went by and Myrtle, Elaine, and Red exchanged dialogue on everything from Red and Elaine's upcoming anniversary to local gossip.

Red finally stopped chatting and watched Miles with concern. "Is the timer a medical thing, Miles? You're doing okay, aren't you?"

Miles seized on this question like it was a life preserver. "As a matter of fact, it *is* a medical thing, yes. I should be taking my medicine now."

Myrtle stared at him. "What medicine is that? You never told me about any medicine." She sounded very put out by the idea that she wouldn't know something important about her friend.

"It's a rather delicate issue that I'd rather not discuss," said Miles with dignity. "I'm perfectly fine. But we do need to leave now so that I can take my medicine."

"Can't you just walk across the street and take it?" asked Myrtle impatiently. "I don't require an escort when I take *my* medicine."

"But I left it at your house," said Miles smoothly as he stood up. "So we should take our leave. Thanks for the visit, Elaine and Red."

As Miles hurried out the door with Myrtle in tow, they could hear Red say to Elaine, "Do you suppose he has diabetes? He's needing to rush home for an injection or to test his blood? Poor guy." And Elaine say in return, "But he seems so healthy! And why would diabetes be a delicate medical issue?"

Miles continued bustling Myrtle up Red and Elaine's walkway until she stopped and gave him a small shove. "What on earth is this nonsense, Miles? You're as healthy as an ox."

"The *casserole*," said Miles with exasperation. "It's about incinerating your casserole. And possibly your house if we don't get a move-on."

Myrtle snapped her fingers. "The squash. Right. So you set a timer on your phone? I can see you didn't trust me to remember my casserole."

"For good reason. I only hope it's salvageable and not too charred. I don't think you have enough makeshift ingredients to cook another one."

"Although we probably have enough squash," said Myrtle.

When they walked inside, the house did have a faint charcoal smell. Miles groaned as they headed toward the kitchen.

Myrtle turned off the oven and peered inside. The casserole sat amid the smokiness, looking quite black on the top where the cheese had been.

"We shouldn't have left it," said Miles with a sigh. "Oh well. At least the squash was properly disposed of. It wasn't as if we threw it away. I hate throwing food away."

Myrtle carefully removed the squash casserole from the oven, placing it with great care on the top of the stove. Then, as if it were second nature to her, she opened all the windows in the kitchen to allow the room to air out. Pasha jumped into the window from the backyard to watch her movements with interest. This also appeared to be part of an all-too-familiar routine.

"It's perfect," she said, beaming at the casserole. "It was ingenious of me to charbroil it, don't you think?"

"Charbroil?" asked Miles. "Is that the new term for burned?"

"No, burned is when it's in ashes," murmured Myrtle, carefully scraping off one particularly burned bit.

"I think charbroil means something very different."

"Blackened then. Everyone is always talking about blackened chicken. Why not blackened squash?"

Miles was looking rather queasy. "The burned squash smell is getting to me. You can present it however you like to the cast. I'll go along with it. But right now I want to escape the fumes."

Myrtle glanced at the rooster clock on the wall. "But we were going to go to the diner and ask Cady some questions."

"I thought the next thing we were going to do was to go to the theater and talk to the cast and hand over the toxic casserole," said Miles.

"The *blackened* casserole," corrected Myrtle. "And the cast practice isn't until suppertime, remember? I was going to briefly heat the casserole up after we got back from the diner."

Miles seemed to wince at the mention of putting the casserole back into the oven. "It's not really even lunchtime yet. I'm going to put my feet up for a while. Let's go over there after the lunch rush is over with. Otherwise, we probably won't even get a chance to talk to Cady because she'll be rushing around getting everyone's orders."

"All right, I guess that will work out okay. So maybe one-thirty? Although I'm not sure how much time I'll have after that to heat the squash casserole back up."

Miles's face was immediately relieved.

ALTHOUGH MYRTLE COULDN'T imagine being able to rest with the excitement of the investigation, she found that she got very, very drowsy during today's episode of *Tomorrow's Promise*. It might have been that the storyline wasn't particularly interesting (did they really need Stefano dumping yet another girlfriend? Wasn't there anything else Stefano could do? Find a job, perhaps? Stop giving strange women meaningful looks that he imagined to be sultry but were actually sulky?), but it might also have been that figuring out mysteries was taxing for the brain. At any rate, Myrtle fell into a deep sleep. Like most felines, Pasha usually liked her personal space. But this afternoon, she crept up while Myrtle was sleeping, gingerly hopped next to her on the recliner, and curled up for a nap.

When Myrtle woke up, she had the alarming sensation, both that a lot of time had passed and she was late for something, and that something living and furry was next to her. Fortunately, she suppressed her instinct to fling herself out of the recliner because Pasha was quite peacefully sleeping next to her. Myrtle squinted at the clock across the room on the desk. It was after one in the afternoon. She'd had a fairly long nap, which boded ill for the quality of her sleeping that night. What was more, Pasha was being so sweet that she felt trapped in her chair. She hated to discourage the feral cat from acting domesticated.

There was a light tap at her door. It must be Miles. "Come in!" she commanded in a yodeling voice, all the while shooting anxious glances at Pasha. But the black cat, clearly exhausted from whatever nocturnal adventures she'd gone on, slept soundly on.

The light tap came again. "*Come in!*" said Myrtle, a bit more forcefully.

The doorknob rattled. "It's not unlocked," said Miles in a reproachful tone.

"Can you come in through the back door? I'm somewhat trapped," said Myrtle.

"Somewhat? All right, I'll give the back door a try."

A minute later, Miles returned to the front door and said, "Your back gate is locked."

Myrtle sighed. Dusty had been most meticulous about locking her gate, ever since there'd been a rash of bodies in her backyard. She ordinarily appreciated it. She opened her mouth to suggest that Miles scale the fence, but then Pasha finally gave a great feline stretch, licked her paw to give herself a post-nap touch-up, and lazily leapt to the floor.

"Do I need to break a window?" asked Miles. "You haven't fallen and broken something, have you? Should I call Red?"

"Oh goodness, *no*. No, I'm free now," said Myrtle as she hurried to the door.

A rather flustered Miles stood at her front door, studying her with concern. "You're all right," he said with some relief.

"Of course I'm all right. Fit as a fiddle. I had a very unexpected nap. And then it became more unexpected when Pasha decided to curl up by me in my chair," said Myrtle. She headed for the desk and her purse.

Miles opened his mouth and then snapped it closed again. Pasha glared at him from the window sill. Her face seemed to say that she didn't think that Miles really *understood* her like Myrtle did.

"So, off to the diner then," said Myrtle. "I'm really getting hungry. I might have to have *two* pimento cheese dogs with chili fries." She paused. "Miles, are you sure you don't need to go see about your stomach? First you turned green at the squash casserole and now you can't seem to handle the thought of a little greasy food."

"I think I'll stick with a salad at Bo's," said Miles. "But before we go, I have some news."

Myrtle said, "News? What kind of news? I thought you went home for a rest."

"I did. But I also got information from a very informed source. This source, who I will protect by providing anonymity, claims that Roscoe Ragsdale and Nandina were having an affair."

Miles beamed and he looked very pleased with himself for supplying information.

Myrtle raised her eyebrows. "An affair! Good work, Miles."

"Although I have a confession to make. I'm not really certain which one Roscoe is."

Myrtle said, "He's the one who's tanned and has big, brown eyes and black, springy hair. He has a few smile lines that complement his general appearance."

"Oh, the one with the scruffy beard," said Miles. He unconsciously rubbed his own clean-shaved face as if testing for any impudent growth.

"It's just a five o'clock shadow," said Myrtle impatiently. "And I wish you'd disclose your source. Maybe we can get some more information out of them."

"I doubt it," said Miles quickly. "This source seemed completely tapped out on everything *he or she* knew."

Myrtle looked at him suspiciously from narrowed eyes. "Hmm."

CHAPTER SIX

THE DINER WASN'T NEARLY as busy this afternoon as it had been yesterday. Parking was ample right in front of the restaurant on the street. The old boys that Miles had seen at the gym that morning had now camped out on the benches at the front of the diner. Miles muttered, "So they went to the gym and now they're having a calorie extravaganza? I thought it was usually another group of old guys that hung out here."

"I'm sure they must think the same thing about us. We appear to be doing the same thing. Except that we didn't exercise," said Myrtle.

"And we won't be eating the high-calorie stuff," said Miles.

"Speak for yourself."

When they opened the door into the diner, Cady was walking by with a tray of food. "Hi!" she said with a grin.

"Hi Cady," said Myrtle. "Where is your section? We wanted to talk to you if you can spare some time."

"Right there," said Cady, gesturing to some tables at the front of the restaurant by the window. "I can probably talk a little, if we're not too obvious about it. It's pretty quiet in here now. Not like earlier."

Miles, who always had a very well-developed work ethic, said with a frown, "We won't get you into trouble, will we?"

Cady grinned at them, "Who cares? If I get fired from this job, there are other jobs waiting tables."

Miles and Myrtle sat in Cady's section to wait for her to finish up. "She seems rather cavalier about her job," said Miles in a disapproving tone.

"Which could indicate other issues. She's cavalier about her job. She's perhaps a little less than totally reliable. Perhaps she lies. Perhaps she even murders people."

Miles raised his eyebrows. "Surely that's a stretch, isn't it?"

"A personality flaw is a personality flaw," said Myrtle with a shrug. "It all depends on how the person with the flaw squashes it down."

"Why do I feel a *Tomorrow's Promise* example coming?" asked Miles, picking up a well-worn laminated menu with a sigh.

"Because they cover the gamut in terms of personalities, flaws, and strengths," said Myrtle promptly. "Remember little Tina?"

Miles's brow wrinkled. "Not so much, no. I do like the show, but all the characters start running together."

"That's what happens when you nap in the middle of the show," said Myrtle severely. She left out the fact that she'd drifted asleep during today's show, since it was an anomaly. "Anyway, Tina's flaw was that she was overly impressed by people with money. Totally distracted by bright, shiny objects. On a small scale, this meant that Tina got involved with the wrong people for the wrong reasons. She was in relationships with men only because they had flashy watches or nice cars."

Miles nodded. "Okay, now I'm remembering Tina. As I recall, she ended up being part of a bank heist. She ran into the bank wearing a pirate costume and carrying a machine gun." He tilted his head thoughtfully to one side. "I never could get over that visual aberration. If she were wearing a pirate costume, shouldn't she have been carrying a sword?"

"Anyway, the important point here is that Tina could have stopped her flaw from exploding out of control. She could have been someone who just found herself in inappropriate relationships instead of someone who found herself in prison. It's how we handle our shortcomings," said Myrtle, tapping the table with her hands emphatically.

"I thought Tina escaped from jail during that prison break episode," said Miles.

"The point is that Cady is a bit lazy and maybe somewhat irresponsible. That could lay the groundwork for other things," said Myrtle. "You're hard to keep on task today, Miles. It's like herding cats."

"But Cady has an alibi. She arrived late to the theater because her car broke down," said Miles.

"Who knows—maybe she had a partner who actually murdered Nandina. And she was only part of it. Okay, shh. Here she comes." Myrtle folded her hands on the table and put her sweetest old lady face on.

"Let me get your order in for you and then I'll sit down for a chat," said Cady, blue eyes twinkling at them. But the bell on the diner door rang and she frowned. "What on earth? There's a huge group coming in."

Myrtle turned in the booth and craned her head to see. "For heaven's sake. It's the old boys from outside!"

Miles shrugged. "They're allowed to eat, surely."

"Not now!" hissed Myrtle.

Cady sighed. "Sorry, that's going to take up some of my time. At least let me get your orders in and then maybe I can have a minute when I'm bringing your food by."

Myrtle ordered her favorite pimento cheese dogs and chili cheese fries and Miles ordered a healthy and entirely un-diner-like salad.

"They're ruining everything!" said Myrtle, staring with eyes like daggers at the old men.

"I'm just glad they didn't choose to sit over here with us," said Miles. "I don't think we could have interviewed Cady with them sitting here."

Their food came, but Cady gave them an apologetic look. "I've still got to bring them their drinks and take their orders."

Once they'd eaten their food the bell on the diner door rang again and Myrtle peered around in irritation. "More people? Where are all these people coming from? Are they purposefully trying to mess up our investigation?"

A different waitress kept coming by to try to take plates away. Myrtle was feeling hurried. "I won't leave until we talk to Cady!"

Miles, who recognized determination when he saw it, settled back and made himself comfortable in his booth. Myrtle kept ordering more drinks in order to better linger. The diner continued filling up with people. "At this rate and with all this lemonade, by the time Cady finally comes over to talk to us, I'll be camped out in the ladies' room."

Finally, everyone who had come in was fed and watered and content and Cady walked to their table. "I hope I'm not putting you too far behind. That was a huge crowd!"

"It was fine," said Myrtle in a hurry, not wanting her to have more customers before she could finish asking her questions. "All we've got today is to go to the cast rehearsal this evening."

Cady's blue eyes opened wide. "Oh, the rehearsal was canceled. Out of respect for Nandina, you know. I just got a text message on it a little while ago."

Myrtle frowned. "Well, pooh. I'd made this casserole for the bereaved cast members. I was going to take it to them when I was there to ask questions."

Cady said, "You could try giving the casserole to Skip. You know him? Skip Rogers. He's planning on being at the theater in about thirty minutes. He's making some sort of makeshift memorial to Nandina outside the theater and invited us all to come by." Her eyes grew dreamy. "Isn't it terribly tragic? He's so painfully grief-stricken."

"Thanks for the heads-up. We'll be there then. And we'll give whoever is there the casserole." Myrtle paused. "Do you think some of the others will be there, too?"

"I doubt it," said Cady, making a face. "Nandina wasn't exactly popular with the rest of the cast."

"Is there anyone in particular who seemed upset with Nandina? Veronica maybe?" asked Myrtle.

"Oh, of course Veronica was furious with Nandina. But that's a professional thing. It's nothing personal. Veronica would have been upset with anyone who was the new, improved version of her. Veronica came into the theater as a starlet. Then she started looking older, you know, losing her looks a little. Next thing you know, she's lost all the romantic lead roles to Nandina." Cady shrugged as if this were all the natural state of affairs.

"Sounds like a motive to me," said Myrtle.

Miles said, "What puzzles me is that Veronica cares so much about being a romantic lead at a community theater in Bradley."

"It's her whole life," said Cady, staring at Miles as if he were completely uncultured. "Even if it's not Broadway or Hollywood. Acting is what keeps her going. But, like I was saying, it wasn't personal. It could have been anybody who was young and pretty and she'd have been just as unhappy."

Myrtle said, "It seemed to me as if Nandina rubbed it in, though. It seemed to me as if it were personal."

Cady shook her head. "No way. Especially not enough to kill her over." She tilted her head thoughtfully. "Although I did see her pinch Nandina once."

"Do adults still pinch?" Myrtle blinked at Cady. "I thought only small children behaved that way."

"Small children who need to spend some serious time in time-out," muttered Miles.

Cady was adamant. "Veronica isn't a killer."

"Then who is?" asked Myrtle persistently. She hadn't drunk a gallon of lemonade to come away with no leads at all.

Cady said, "Have you thought about talking to Blaine? I think he and Nandina were having an affair."

"An affair?" parroted Myrtle.

"Yes," said Cady. A wistful look passed across her features. Cady clearly was a Blaine admirer. Despite the fact that she'd basically labeled him as a suspect.

Cady glanced over at the other tables and heaved a tremendous sigh. "I've got to check in on everyone. Sorry."

And she was gone.

Miles said, "Was that even helpful?"

They were heading back to Myrtle's house to heat up the casserole.

"I suppose," said Myrtle slowly. "Although I'd already seen evidence that Blaine and Nandina might have been having a fling. `The handholding that was going on under the table at the diner."

"At least it was corroborated by Cady. I'd hate to think my arteries are under such pressure for nothing," said Miles.

"They're hardly under pressure when all you eat at the diner are salads. Your arteries are probably pining for some real excitement."

A few minutes later they were back in Myrtle's kitchen. Miles raised his eyebrows as Myrtle preheated the oven to 450 degrees F. "Myrtle, in the interest of casserole preservation, it might make more sense for the oven to be set at something like 200 degrees."

"We don't have enough time to slowly reheat. Not today. After the entire world showed up at Bo's Diner it put us quite a bit behind."

Miles and Myrtle watched the parts of *Tomorrow's Promise* that Myrtle had slept through earlier. Myrtle was relieved to see that the storylines got better. In fact, they were so engrossed in Marlena and Greg being stranded on a desert island that seemed to be inhabited by an odd tribe of malevolent giants, that they blinked at each other in surprise at the acrid smell of something burning.

Myrtle hurried into the kitchen and rushed to the oven. She put on her bright red oven mitts and carefully pulled out the casserole.

"Wow," said Miles from the kitchen door.

"I know," said Myrtle, staring at the casserole. "It was accidental genius, wasn't it? Serendipity. It looks *especially* blackened, now. As if a professional painstakingly turned the dish to get the blacking all over the squash."

"I don't think a professional had anything to do with this process. And I'm not sure that we should foist this creation on unsuspecting Skip. Not if we want to keep him around. I wasn't even a fan of this casserole *before* it was cooked," said Miles.

"It's perfectly fine. It's the gourmet nature of the blackening that makes you uneasy, that's all. Your stomach leans toward simpler fare, Miles. We're going to put some extra feta on the top and all will be well." Myrtle quickly dumped the rest of the cheese on the top of the casserole and spread it out with a fork.

Then she covered it back up with foil and glanced up at the clock. "We need to go right now. Otherwise we might miss Skip at the theater."

"Poor Skip," said Miles as they walked to the car. "I feel as if I need to put a warning label on the casserole dish."

Myrtle ignored him. "I feel rather sorry for Skip, myself. He clearly cared for Nandina. But, although I've now heard that

Nandina wasn't picky about being romantically involved with a couple of the cast members, it sounds as if he wasn't one of them."

"He's not in the same league as Blaine or Roscoe," said Miles. "Not in terms of looks, anyway. And Nandina seems like the sort of person who would go for a flashier type of man."

When they arrived at the theater, they saw Skip Rogers sitting on the ground next to the building. He'd apparently just finished creating the makeshift memorial and was staring at his handiwork. It consisted of several heart balloons, a card that said *Nandina* on it in large letters, and scattered roses. When he heard the car engine get close, the young man looked up eagerly, as though he was glad to see another cast member at his memorial. When he spotted Myrtle and Miles, he turned back around and his shoulders slumped.

It all seemed to make Miles rather uncomfortable. He shifted in his seat. "We're not spending long here, are we? I hate intruding on someone's grief." He looked at the entire scene in front of him with a grimace.

"Only until he provides us information in exchange for the casserole," said Myrtle, removing her seatbelt.

Skip blinked in surprise as Myrtle and Miles approached him. He stood slowly. "Hi. Are you friends of Nandina's?" His eyes were doubtful as he took in Myrtle's and Miles's gray hairs. And the white ones.

"We're friends of the arts," said Myrtle briskly. "I'm Myrtle Clover and this is Miles Bradford. We were in the audience at last night's performance. It was devastating. Miles and I wanted to come and offer our condolences to the cast."

"I'm afraid the cast isn't here right now. Although they should be. Practice was canceled tonight and I tried to get everyone to come out and celebrate Nandina's life. You can see how much they cared." His voice was bitter.

"Well, *we* care," said Myrtle in a hearty voice. "We brought a casserole. A consolatory gesture, you know. Since no one else is here to receive it, we think you should be the one to have it."

Miles shuddered and Myrtle glanced reprovingly at him.

Skip gave Myrtle a shy smile. "Thank you! I really appreciate it. You, at least, understand."

Myrtle was about to gently ask Skip who he thought could have been responsible for Nandina's death when he suddenly volunteered the information on his own. "This is Roscoe's doing. I'm sure of it."

Myrtle tilted her head thoughtfully. "What makes you think that Roscoe had anything to do with this?" She studiously avoided Miles's face. He looked very smug since his "source" had been corroborated. Whoever his source was.

"I know that Roscoe's wife, Josie, *definitely* thought that Nandina and Roscoe were having an affair. She kept showing up and hanging out in the parking lot during practice. I'm sure she was trying to catch the two of them together," said Skip.

Miles said, "Did Roscoe's wife have a good reason to think her husband was involved with Nandina?"

"Or was she just a very jealous person who suspected her husband was involved with *everyone*?"

Skip said, "I don't know what made her think that. And I don't know for sure if they were having an affair. But I kept seeing them having these illicit conversations."

Myrtle raised her eyebrows. "How do you know they were illicit? What made them illicit instead of simply regular conversations?"

"Their attitudes. They were acting furtively. You know, quick conversations in deserted back hallways in the theater. Talking intently in a car before practice started or after it ended." Skip shrugged to show he didn't care, but his face reflected his hurt.

"But why would *Roscoe* have wanted to kill Nandina if he were having an affair with her?" asked Myrtle.

Skip shrugged again, but this time his face was thoughtful. "I don't know. Maybe Nandina broke up with him and he was upset about that?"

Myrtle said, "Or maybe Josie was responsible. Maybe she was furious about her husband's affair and decided to get rid of Nandina."

"But how would Roscoe's wife end up onstage to murder Nandina?" asked Miles, spreading his hands out in front of him.

"Oh, that would have been easy," said Skip quickly. "The back entrance is always unlocked. And it was dark onstage. She could have been hiding in the dressing area or in one of the storage rooms where we keep old sets and costumes. It wouldn't have been hard for her to slip by in dark clothes while everyone else was scurrying around during a set change."

"That actually makes a lot of sense," said Miles, nodding. Myrtle could tell he'd made up his mind. Lately it seemed like Miles always had a pet suspect for every case.

He'd even convinced Skip. Myrtle could see the young man's eyes darken. She quickly said, "Just because something makes sense doesn't mean that it's so." Then she asked Skip intently, "Where were you when Nandina died? Did you see anything at all?"

Skip shook his head, a regretful look crossing his features. "Not a thing. Oh, I was onstage when it happened, and of course I was the one who discovered her death. But, like the rest of the cast, I was running around like a chicken with my head cut off. We had a lot of things to move around and the stuff was heavy. It was awkward to move, even though it was on casters. We were moving out the living room furniture from the first scene and turning it into a bedroom. Nandina's bed was the first part of that set that was moved in."

"So there was plenty of time for someone to murder Nandina," said Myrtle.

"Plenty of time," repeated Skip. "And the whole cast was involved in the set change because small productions like this one have to have all hands on deck."

"Anyone had the opportunity to murder her, then," said Miles.

"What was Nandina like before the show?" asked Myrtle. "Did she act differently at all?"

Skip frowned. "Do you mean, nervous at all? Scared? She didn't. She was brimming with confidence, as usual. Drinking her customary glass of wine before the curtain rose. Smiling at everyone. Excited about the performance. Sunny." He teared up.

Myrtle knew when it was time to leave. She cleared her throat. "Miles, I think we should be heading back now."

Skip tried to recover. "Thanks so much for the casserole."

Miles made a choking sound and hurried off for the safety of the car.

CHAPTER SEVEN

"WHERE ARE WE GOING now?" asked Miles, stifling a yawn.

"To the library, before it closes," said Myrtle, buckling her seatbelt with a decisive click.

"The library?" Miles frowned. "Can't your errands wait until tomorrow? I'm feeling pretty wiped out. I didn't get a nap today like you did."

"Josie works at the library. We'll seize the opportunity to interview her before she leaves for the day," said Myrtle as Miles started driving away from the theater.

"Won't she tell us to be quiet?" asked Miles uneasily. "I don't want to get into any trouble."

"Which only goes to show that you haven't visited our local library lately. A pity. I'm there nearly every day. If I'm not checking out more books, I'm reading magazines. The library is bustling these days and certainly not quiet. There are children's programs and classes on learning to use a computer. And study groups. It's a very popular place that isn't silent," said Myrtle.

Miles gave her a reproachful look. "You know I'm a huge reader. I usually purchase my books, though, because I like to underline passages and write in the margins. Libraries don't approve of marginalia."

But Myrtle had already tuned out and was thinking about the suspects again. "I wonder who wasn't involved with Nandina. So far we've heard about Blaine and Roscoe."

"Don't forget Skip," said Miles.

"Skip wasn't involved with Nandina. He only wanted to be, which is, in itself, a motive. An unrequited love sort of thing."

"I think Josie is behind Nandina's death," said Miles. There was a deep-seated conviction in his voice. "It makes the most sense. She was the one who was most upset at Nandina."

"I'm not sure that's true. Here, park right in front," said Myrtle, waving her hand at a spot at the very front of the library.

Miles seemed reluctant to get out of the car. "I'm assuming that we're not just going into the library and accusing the resident librarian of murder. Do we have a plan for getting information from Josie? Particularly since we don't have a casserole to soften her up?"

Myrtle frowned. "I was just going to tell her that we were investigating for the newspaper and wanted to talk with her about Nandina."

"Then it really won't be quiet in the library. I have a feeling that we need to ease into our conversation with Josie a little more. You're in super sleuth mode and she's unsuspecting. It might not go well. How about if I ask her for a book recommendation? Then maybe you can eventually ask about the murder," said Miles.

Myrtle was already opening the car door and stepping out. "Fine, fine. If that's how you want to handle it. But I can't beat around the bush too long because the library is closing soon."

They hurried up the concrete steps, through an atrium, and then through a set of glass doors to the library. Myrtle peered to the left at the circulation desk. "She's not manning the circulation desk. Pooh."

"Maybe she's not working tonight," suggested Miles.

Myrtle's narrowed eyes bode ill for Josie if she wasn't working.

"Maybe she's in the stacks, shelving books. That must be a huge part of her day, you know. Let's wander through the books," said Miles.

Wandering through the books would usually be music to Myrtle's ears, but she was very task-oriented today. They started in biographies, proceeded to young adult, and were in the Ms of general fiction when they saw her.

"She certainly does play the part of a librarian," said Miles in a low voice.

Myrtle murmured, "Most librarians aren't like the cliché at all. But I think that's exactly what she's doing—playing a part. She doesn't have to work, she's fairly attractive. And yet she's wearing blue stockings. Literally wearing blue hose. She'd do well to go on the stage, herself."

They walked up to the thin young woman who was dressed severely in a baggy cardigan and shapeless skirt with blue stockings underneath. Miles said politely, "I was wondering if you could help me find something to read."

Josie turned and gave him a prim smile. "Of course. What kinds of books do you like to read?"

"I'm particularly fond of the classics, but I think I'd like to branch into some solid historical fiction. Nothing too outlandish. Nothing where history is rewritten. Nothing where the author steps out of the time period to judge the characters based on 21st century standards."

Myrtle gave Miles an alarmed frown. He appeared to be warming to his task too much. In fact, it seemed as though he were giving the local library a go. Which she'd ordinarily approve of, but not when they were trying to interview suspects before the library closed for the evening.

Josie was leading them through the aisles of books. "Here's one you might enjoy. Low on sentimentality. And here's another with a nice storyline but a very matter-of-fact retelling and some strong character development."

Myrtle, who'd been looking for a segue, said, "Speaking of characters, I believe your husband is an actor, isn't he? Roscoe?"

Josie gave them a very cold look. "He acts, yes."

She seemed to be waiting for Myrtle to continue, and so Myrtle obliged. "Miles and I were at the theater last night and saw Roscoe in action. He's a great actor." This was perhaps a bit of an exaggeration. He was clearly very passionate about his acting, but his acting had distracted Myrtle. He overacted. And overacting always took Myrtle out of the story.

Josie might have thought Myrtle was exaggerating, too. "Hmph."

Myrtle continued, "Such a terrible tragedy last night, too. I'm sure it must have been very upsetting to all of the cast. My son is the police chief and he said it was definitely murder. Who do you think could have done such a thing?"

Miles looked gravely through his rimless glasses at Myrtle. She could tell he thought she was pushing for too much information too quickly. But the library was about to close. And now they also had to leave enough time for Miles to check his books out.

Josie grew even stiffer, if that were possible and seemed to pale at the words *police officer*. She reared herself up to her full height, which was about five inches shorter than Myrtle's. Still, the effect was quite off-putting. It was definitely a 'back off' look.

"You're not implying that Roscoe had anything to do with it, I hope."

"I wouldn't dream of it," said Myrtle with her best shocked-old-lady look, hand to her heart. "But do you have any idea who might have done it? Considering how much you know about the theater and the cast."

Myrtle hoped that she might be buttering Josie up, but she seemed completely insulted that Myrtle thought she was involved at all with the theater. "Absolutely not! It's not one of my hangouts, you know. Sometimes I see Roscoe's performances, but that's the extent of my knowledge of the theater. And I was nowhere near the theater last night. Who'd want to see a play called *Malaise*?"

Miles fumbled and nearly dropped his library books at the icy quality of Josie's voice and she leveled a reproving glare at him.

Myrtle wheedled, "Maybe that Blaine though. Does he seem like someone who might have wanted Nandina out of the way? Or maybe Skip?"

Josie snapped in a voice much too loud for a librarian, "All I know is that Roscoe wouldn't have harmed a hair on Nandina's head. Not a hair. You can go tell your son that. The *idea* of him sending his elderly mother out to do his investigating for him!"

Miles glanced around the library nervously at the loudness of Josie's voice.

The last thing Myrtle wanted was for Josie to go blabbing to Red with complaints. She said calmly, "Red has nothing to do with this. I'm interested in the case myself. I report on crime for the Bradley Bugle, you know. And I wasn't trying to point the finger at Roscoe—I was trying to get leads."

Josie seemed to relax a little. Or, at least, her fingers weren't picking apart the hem of her cardigan any longer. She even started looking thoughtful instead of defensive. Slowly she said, "I was being truthful when I said that I don't know much about the cast. That's Roscoe's thing and I'm just indulging him in it. But I have noticed that one of the women there, Veronica, I think she's called, had been very resentful toward Nandina. She felt like Nandina had all the good lines and that Nandina had more lines and that she was being slowly forced out. Since she'd been something of a star there, I gather this has been particularly traumatic for her." Josie shrugged as if not being able to completely comprehend it. "Veronica used to consider herself this sort of femme fatale. But Nandina's appearance on the scene completely changed everything."

Myrtle was about to ask a few more questions about Veronica when Josie said abruptly, "And now it's time for you to check those books out. The circulation desk will be closing down soon." And Josie disappeared down another aisle.

Miles seemed relieved. "She's a very intense woman," he whispered, still trying to maintain his standards regarding the appropriate volume level at a public library.

"It makes me wonder," said Myrtle. "That intensity could be applied toward other things. Like jealousy. And murder. Just like Cady's flaws. And Tina's from *Tomorrow's Promise.*"

Miles stood in front of the circulation desk, frowning. "Well, this is inconvenient. No one is here to check out my books."

"Just use the self-service checkout," said Myrtle impatiently. "It's why it's there."

Miles hesitantly pulled out his wallet, found his library card (with some difficulty), and then proceeded to scan the card upside-down.

"For heaven's sake," muttered Myrtle. She took the card and books from him and quickly checked him out. "You probably don't use the self-checkout at the grocery store, either."

Miles said stiffly, "Only because I buy a lot of produce. And I never can read the tiny print of the produce code on the stickers."

Myrtle sighed. "I'm sorry, Miles. I'm prickly today and I think it's because nothing has gone according to plan. Lunch at the diner was crazy, not quiet. The practice was canceled. And Josie was a hostile witness."

"Still, I think we got useful information," said Miles, opening the door for Myrtle as they left the library. "And the best part of it all is that I'm completely exhausted. Maybe, finally, I'll be able to get some sleep."

Myrtle didn't sleep nearly as well that night, which she blamed on her unusual nap during *Tomorrow's Promise*. Since she knew Miles believed he would be able to sleep, she didn't head over to his house for a middle of the night coffee. Instead, she threw back the bedsheets, pulled on her robe and slippers, and decided to do a crossword puzzle. Sometimes crosswords relaxed her when nothing else did.

Twenty minutes later, however, Myrtle decided that this particular crossword puzzle wasn't relaxing at all. In fact, it appeared to have been designed by an evil genius intent on avoiding *any* common crossword puzzle words. No *era*? No *Erie* or *oleo*? Not one appearance from *irate*? Really? She'd half a mind to write the puzzle designer a letter.

As she was scowling at the newspaper, she spotted something in her peripheral vision. It was dust. There appeared to be a dust convention taking place at the baseboard near her fireplace. The tables also looked as though they could use a dusting. Myrtle tried to remember the last time she'd successfully been able to compel Puddin to clean. Puddin was just as determined not to come and clean as Myrtle was determined to have her come by. Puddin's stock excuse was that her back was thrown, although she'd recently branched into a brand new excuse: that she had to go to the store to buy more cleaning supplies. But, since she always used Myrtle's supplies, that excuse held no water for Myrtle, and Puddin knew it. She'd have loved to have taken

Miles up on his offer to have Wanda stand in for Puddin. But circumstances prevented that little dream from becoming reality.

Myrtle checked the clock, thinking that perhaps it was later in the morning than she thought. Unfortunately, the clock indicated that it was five a.m. Myrtle made a face. She certainly wouldn't get a response if she called Puddin at this hour.

A tap on the door made Myrtle jump and then stare thoughtfully at the door. Miles? But he'd been genuinely tired. Maybe Red. Sometimes he'd be up very early for work and would see Myrtle's lights on and come in for a coffee. But when Myrtle opened the door, she stared in shock at the pale, dumpy person on her doorstep. Puddin.

"Puddin!" Myrtle rubbed her eyes. Had the crossword put her to sleep and she was now dreaming? "What on earth are you doing here?"

"Couldn't sleep," said Puddin spitefully. She looked up at Myrtle with her small eyes. "Spendin' too much time with *you*, I guess."

"Insomnia isn't catching, you know."

Puddin didn't deign to answer this statement. She heaved in a tote bag that appeared to have cleaning supplies in it. Myrtle blinked at the display of rags and glass cleaners and floor cleaners and gloves. "Now I know I *must* be dreaming."

Puddin kicked the door shut behind her and set about unpacking a few items from the tote.

Myrtle said, "Now, Dusty didn't come with you, did he? Because cleaning inside at five a.m. is one thing. Making a racket with a weed trimmer right across from the police chief might just put Dusty in the slammer."

Puddin said, "Dusty is sleepin.'"

"No surprise there," muttered Myrtle. She walked back over to her chair and sat gingerly down. "I feel as if I'm entering the Twilight Zone. Wanda has money? Puddin has cleaning supplies and a work ethic?"

"Naw, Puddin can't *sleep!*" said Puddin, relentlessly resentful. "Told the doctor and he said to exercise."

Myrtle wasn't about to tell Puddin that the gentleman had probably intended her to get her heart rate up. And Puddin's cleaning, at least as far as Myrtle had been able to witness, wouldn't raise her heart rate a bit.

"Where did all your cleaning supplies come from?" asked Myrtle as Puddin studiously put on gloves and started spraying every flat surface with a tremendous amount of furniture polish.

"Mr. Miles done gave them to me," she said.

"*What?*"

If there was one thing she didn't like, it was that from time to time Puddin would clean Miles's house. The thing she disliked most about it is that Puddin seemed to do a most respectable job at it. Another thing she disliked was that it made it even more difficult to get on Puddin's cleaning schedule.

"Mr. Miles did. As a present." She gave Myrtle a simpering smile.

This made Myrtle think. Puddin had brand-new supplies. Miles had carefully *not* told Myrtle about Puddin recently cleaning for him. Miles had a new informant who seemed to have information about Roscoe and Nandina. And Miles was determined to hide the identity of this person. Puddin was both nosy and an eavesdropper and also had a penchant for gossip. The only reasonable conclusion to draw was:

"Puddin, have you been talking to Miles about this murder?" Myrtle's eyes narrowed.

Dust flew up from a table as Puddin hit the surface with a squirt of cleaner. She turned a smug expression to Myrtle. "I had information for him. Mr. Miles likes information."

"You know you can always give *me* information, Puddin. I'm your regular employer, you know," said Myrtle with great irritation.

"I ain't been cleaning real regular lately," said Puddin. She slapped a rag around the table, leaving a puddle of lemon furniture cleaner.

"Which is hardly *my* fault! You haven't returned my phone calls!"

"My back was thrown," said Puddin succinctly.

Myrtle gritted her teeth. She knew from past dealings with Puddin that reasoning with her was like trying to reason with a particularly obtuse toddler. Instead, she attempted to wheedle the information out of her in the hopes of distracting her from her destructive cleaning. She didn't like the idea of her wood furniture being damaged under Puddin's less-than-tender care.

"Tell me what you know, then. What you told Miles. Something about Roscoe and Nandina being an item, right? How did you know about that?" asked Myrtle.

It worked. Puddin, considering her reply, was much more thoughtful and less haphazard in her cleaning. "I saw them together in the parking lot. Sometimes I help Mr. Toucan out at the theater. Cleanin' you know."

Having witnessed the theater's cleanliness, or lack thereof, firsthand, Myrtle could believe that. "So you saw them ... embracing?"

Puddin shook her head. "There wasn't no embracing. They was fightin'."

"Fighting? How close were you?"

"Close enough to tell they was fightin', not huggin'," said Puddin emphatically.

"So why did this make you think that they were having an affair?" Myrtle watched Puddin work on another table in exasperation.

Puddin said scornfully, "Lovers' quarrel! Plain as the nose on your face!" She finally finished torturing Myrtle's tables, replaced the furniture cleaner, took out some floor cleaner, and plodded into the kitchen.

Myrtle got up from her chair and followed Puddin, frowning. "I'm not so sure. They might not have been having an affair at all. They might have been having an argument on any number of different things."

"In a car? Sittin' so close?" scoffed Puddin.

"If they were having an argument in a car, they'd *have* to be close. It sounds to me as if it's more likely that they were just trying to have a private conversation." Myrtle wondered if Josie had also reached an inaccurate conclusion. If she'd also witnessed them together and gotten the wrong impression.

Puddin was bored with the novelty of having information. And, she was also looking bored with housekeeping, which boded ill for destroying the dust bunnies in Myrtle's living room. "Who knows?" she muttered. Her small eyes glanced up at the pot of coffee on the counter. "Can I have a cup of that?"

After a cup of coffee, however, Puddin somehow became sluggish. The sluggishness occurred right before it was time to take care of the floors. Puddin glanced around her and said abruptly, "I'm tired now. Going to try to sleep again. Got more houses to clean later."

Myrtle sighed and watched as Puddin packed her supplies carefully into her bag and pulled open Myrtle's front door. And shrieked.

Pasha the black cat darted in as Puddin scrambled out of the way. Since Puddin was morbidly afraid of Pasha, Myrtle assumed that the cat's appearance had precipitated the shriek. But when her housekeeper's eyes were still trained in horror out the door, Myrtle walked briskly toward her. "What on earth is it, Puddin?"

Puddin turned toward her and shrugged wordlessly, eyes open as far as they could be to let Myrtle know she found the visitor, whoever it was, most suspicious.

"It's me," croaked a voice from the darkness on the front porch.

"Wanda? Is that you? Is everyone determined to go visiting in the middle of the night tonight? Come on in."

Puddin, despite her own appearance and background, was one of the snobbier people Myrtle knew. "It's okay, Puddin," said Myrtle impatiently. "She's my friend."

Puddin looked most doubtful at this, but obediently moved out of the door frame. Because of her ample girth, this meant she headed *out* instead of stepping aside.

CHAPTER EIGHT

WANDA EMERGED FROM the shadows of the front porch. To Myrtle's alarm, she appeared to be toting a large, brown grocery bag. She paused for a moment and said with a serious look at Puddin, "Never mind about not sleepin'. It'll end soon enough."

She proceeded into the house as Puddin gave Myrtle a meaningful look and mouthed *witches!* At her. At that moment, Pasha chose to wind herself lovingly around Wanda's thin legs. Which likely only solidified Puddin's opinion of Wanda.

Myrtle waved goodbye emphatically and pointedly to Puddin and turned to the scrawny psychic. "Wanda dear. And Pasha, too! You've made an impression on my feral friend." Myrtle petted Pasha, crooning. Then she straightened to give Wanda's bag a wary look.

"Wanted to bring more," said Wanda. She set the bag on Myrtle's coffee table and looked at it with satisfaction.

"More squash?" asked Myrtle. She was glad Miles wasn't here. She'd have hated to see the expression on his face.

Wanda grinned at her, revealing a collection of crooked, missing, and yellowed teeth. "To thank Miles. You'll give it to him? I know he's sleepin' now."

How Wanda could know that Miles was sleeping and not know of his intense hatred of squash, Myrtle wasn't sure. Wanda's odd gift certainly seemed uneven. "I'll see that he gets it. But I'm shocked you have so much *more* harvested, considering how much you brought us yesterday."

"Bumper crop," said Wanda. She sat down on Myrtle's sofa and gently stroked Pasha, who had immediately jumped into her lap.

"Oh good, you can visit," said Myrtle. Although all this activity so early in the morning might mean that Myrtle would have to compensate with a late-morning nap.

"Also brought in some work," Wanda reached into a pocket and pulled out a wrinkled piece of paper. She squinted at it. "Dan helped me with some of the words. Sorry. Hope you get the gist."

Myrtle walked over to get the paper and then sat on the sofa. She had little hope that Crazy Dan, Wanda's aptly named brother, would be much help. And, indeed, the horoscope was nearly incomprehensible for a variety of different reasons from the deplorable penmanship to the ghastly grammar. But the core of the content seemed solid, if odd. Everything from *Skorpeos shudnt eat hambergers frum Hungrey Billys ... espeshelly Mark Tipple* to *Airez need to git there teeth cheked ...that means little Pattie Barnhill.*

"Ah, excellent," said Myrtle diplomatically. "I'll be sure to clean this up. And, perhaps, to delete any references to anything that might provoke a lawsuit for libel."

This seemed to agitate Wanda. "Mark Tipple is gonna get food poisoning from Hungry Billy's," she said.

"That may well be, but I don't think we can *print* something like that. And next time, we should probably consider removing personal references altogether," said Myrtle. Her head started hurting just a bit. This was going to end up being a time consuming project. She rapidly shifted gears before Wanda could plead her case on individual horoscopes. "While you're here, have you got more insights on the case for me?"

Wanda gave her a sideways look with her dark eyes. "Yer in danger."

"Besides that one!"

"Tattletales," said Wanda. She bobbed her head in emphasis and her straggly black hair, liberally interspersed with white swept forward.

Myrtle nodded. She was used to Wanda's pithy visions. Pithy and usually enigmatic. This one had possibilities. Who was the tattletale? Myrtle had a feeling it might be Nandina. In murder investigations, tattletales frequently ended up dead. She'd have to ask Red if Nandina was a blackmailer.

Myrtle said, "Thanks. Nothing else?" Wanda shrugged a shoulder and Myrtle sighed. "Well, we have to make do with what we've got." She watched as Pasha completely forgot she was feral and loved on Wanda and Wanda's nicotine-stained hands scratched the black cat under its chin. "You're up awfully early. I'm getting so many nocturnal visitors that I'm starting to consider my insomnia normal."

"Dan needed the car later," said Wanda in her gravelly voice. "Wanted to get the squash to Miles."

"Oh yes, the squash. He'll certainly be excited about that." Myrtle tried to input no irony whatsoever in her voice as she said it. Somehow, Wanda still gave her a knowing look. She'd have sworn the woman knew Miles didn't like the squash. That Wanda had her own agenda for coming over.

"Wanda, I was about to fix myself a bit of breakfast. Would you like to have some with me?" Although she wasn't entirely sure what in her refrigerator and pantry would qualify as breakfast food, she knew that Wanda wasn't likely to be picky.

"Love some," said Wanda. "Eggs is easy. You can throw all kinds of things into eggs."

Myrtle gave her a thoughtful look at her prescience. "Indeed you can. In fact, perhaps you know better than I do the contents of my pantry?"

Wanda did. And was happy to create an original meal out of the odds and ends in Myrtle's kitchen.

WHEN MILES ARRIVED around ten a.m., Myrtle felt as though it was much later in the day than it was. Miles, on the other hand, looked fresh as a daisy. He looked as though he meant business—a serious sidekick in a white button-down shirt, red tie, and dark pants.

"Breakfast, Miles?" asked Myrtle as she opened the door. Although she devoutly hoped that she was not going to have to eat again since Wanda's lavish spread earlier had filled her up more than she expected. Must have been all the olives she sprinkled in the eggs. They took seats in the living room and Myrtle found her coffee mug and took another sip. Tepid. She'd have to make more.

"Not for me, thanks. I'm fit as a fiddle this morning. Amazing what a good night's sleep can do for you."

Myrtle growled, "All right, no need to rub it in. I'm having to make do on coffee and adrenaline." And, because she was still annoyed by her suspicion that Puddin was cleaning Miles's house, she added with a touch of malevolence, "By the way, a present came in for you this morning."

"For me?" Miles raised his eyebrows. "I wasn't aware it was time for another birthday."

Myrtle motioned to the grocery bag that was still on her coffee table. Miles stood up from his spot on the sofa, peered inside, and gasped. "Is this left over from yesterday? I thought we'd gotten rid of it all!"

"We did. Wanda thoughtfully brought more this morning, especially for you. She asked me to give it to you. She said she was having a bumper crop."

Miles opened his mouth to speak and then snapped it shut again.

"You know, it's really very sweet of Wanda. She clearly wants to pay you back for all your kindness," said Myrtle.

Miles was still staring at the huge bag of squash as he sank back on the sofa. "I never expected to be paid back. Especially not in squash. If she's psychic, how is it possible she's unaware of my squash antipathy?"

"She always reminds us that 'that's not how the sight works.' I imagine she thinks you're absolutely delighted to be the recipient of her squash harvest," said Myrtle, hiding a smile.

"I don't suppose we can somehow sneak up there in the middle of the night and vandalize her crops, can we? Deal it some sort of fatal blow? Spray weed killer? Burn it down?" Miles asked wistfully.

"Certainly not. She's so pleased that she's helping to pay you back. We should allow her to feel good about it. There's probably not a whole lot in her life that she *does* feel good about," said Myrtle.

Miles nodded miserably. "You're right. I know you're right. So what's the plan with this stuff? How do we unload it? Because my conscience won't allow me to throw food away."

"I'm thinking the last casserole we did was such a success that we should make more. And distribute it to the cast when we're there during their practice," said Myrtle.

Miles said, "I object to most of what you just said. I object to the pronoun usage, the fact that the casserole was in any way a success, and that we should even consider inflicting more casseroles on more unsuspecting people."

"Skip was very pleased to get the casserole!"

"Yes, but Skip hadn't tried it yet," said Miles.

"I suppose," said Myrtle irritably. "But I still say fresh produce is a nice thing to share. We'll bring the squash, as-is, to the practice this evening."

"Who are our targets for tonight? Who's left?" asked Miles.

"We have Roscoe Ragsdale and Veronica Parsley. I'm going to try to keep our questioning quiet, so we don't set off any alarm bells with the other suspects. Perhaps we can catch Roscoe on the way into practice and then see Veronica before she leaves. I'm going to stress my role as journalist to Veronica because I think she'll respond well to the press. I'm not sure about Roscoe, though. Maybe I'll just present him with the squash and tell him to distribute it to the cast. Then I can subtly move into some questions," said Myrtle.

"Subtle will be key," said Miles. "I think he might get his back up like Josie did. They seem like two peas in a pod, even if Roscoe *is* straying."

"Speaking of straying," said Myrtle sternly, "I understand you've been straying from your usual housekeeper to my Puddin."

Miles looked both vastly annoyed at being caught out and startled. "I suppose Puddin must have said something. She's already been here? Surely that's very un-Puddin-like to show up so early to work."

"You're avoiding the subject, Miles. Why is Puddin cleaning your house? You know I have a hard enough time scheduling her without more competition." Myrtle scowled at her friend. "What's more, your house is excessively tidy and doesn't require any additional cleaning. I blame your stint in the military for your obsessive organization and cleanliness."

"Puddin is cleaning my house because she does a good job. I have no idea why she does such a poor job cleaning your house or why it's so hard to get her to come over. Perhaps it has something to do with *that*." Miles looked askance at Pasha, who had just uncurled herself and stretched as she lay in a sunbeam on the floor of the living room.

"Pasha is smart enough to keep out of Puddin's way, believe me." Myrtle paused. "It appears that Puddin is also acting as an informant for you."

Miles said, "Only because she was gossiping, as usual. This time she actually had something to say that I was interested in." He looked at the clock. "Now that I've checked in over here, I should run a few errands before we resume our investigating this evening. Do you need anything while I'm out? Like whatever was on your original grocery list?"

Myrtle sighed. "I think Puddin must have thrown away the list in the throes of her cleaning frenzy. And, since she even dumped the trash in the dumpster, I can't fish it out. I'm not much in the mood to recreate the list now, but if I think of something, I'll let you know. I think I'd better check in with Sloan to make sure he knows that I'm the one writing the story on the murder. I saw him yesterday when I was getting Wanda employed, but I didn't have a chance to talk to him about it."

"I thought I saw it in this morning's paper," said Miles with a frown.

"You did. But that was just the basic news article. Mine will be an in-depth article full of quotes from suspects, background information, and whatever I've been able to dig up. You know, the type of investigative treatment I give all my stories."

"Speaking of Wanda—how did that go?" asked Miles a bit anxiously. "Looking at the bag of squash, I'm assuming it went well."

"He hired her," said Myrtle with a shrug. "It was on my recognizance. Basically, I told him I'd make sure the horoscopes would be fine. And, in fact, Wanda included her very first column with the squash." She reached for the scrap of paper from the coffee table and handed it to Miles.

He grimaced. "This is nothing like the old horoscopes! They were usually upbeat and jaunty and applied to most of the town. These are gloomy and vaguely disturbing and specific!"

"Yes, well, we all have things to work on," said Myrtle. "I'm sure Wanda's horoscopes will be the talk of the town. After I work on them, of course. Which I'm doing as soon as you leave. I'll bring the revised copy to Sloan when I visit him."

"A good thing. All right, I'm leaving for now. Let's say four o'clock then," said Miles.

As soon as Miles had left, Myrtle sat down to work on the horoscopes. It was something of a grueling process. First she translated the predictions into Standard English, without regard to content. Then she set about removing any potentially libelous references to local businesses. With some hesitation, she decided to leave in the statements that were meant for one recipient. After all, it was what made Wanda's column different from the rest. Then she grabbed her cane and struck out for downtown Bradley. With any luck, Sloan would be in the newsroom and she could inform him of her intentions.

It really was a beautiful day. Despite her lack of sleep, Myrtle had zip in her step and her cane barely even touched the ground. She beamed at small children on tricycles along the way. Butterflies floated past her on the light breeze on their way to blooming bushes alongside the quiet street. Everything felt good and right and as it should be to Myrtle. Aside from the murder, of course.

Considering a murder had occurred only a couple of days ago, the newspaper office should certainly be open and Sloan should be hard at work. Sloan, as Myrtle had explained to Wanda, did care a lot about the *Bradley Bugle*. But he was also very fond of going out for a beer and a slice of pizza for lunch. And, depending on what kind of day he was having, that lunch could extend into the afternoon. He'd taken now to giving keys out to the various columnists he had on staff at the paper. Myrtle knew that the Good Neighbors columnist had one and even Miss Frozzle, who did the gardening piece every Saturday. It was most annoying that Sloan hadn't thought to give *Myrtle* a key. It made her feel as if he didn't want her wandering around the newsroom.

So, when Myrtle tried the brass doorknob on the weathered wooden door, she was relieved when it opened. She squinted into the cool darkness of the newsroom as her eyes adjusted to the light. Sure enough, there was Sloan, slouched over a desk in a tee shirt that didn't quite cover all of his girth. And . . . a pair of shorts?

Sloan leapt up guiltily as he spotted Myrtle. No matter what he was doing, he always appeared to feel at least somewhat guilty about it.

"Getting ready to leave and go walk," he explained, looking down with a grimace at his shorts and tee shirt and yanking at the hem of the shirt. "Trying to get a little exercise you know. Lose a little weight." He gestured at his desk where the sad remains of a salad were in evidence.

"It's very nice out there," said Myrtle. "It's lucky I caught you before you left, though. I wanted to hand in Wanda's horoscope for tomorrow. And I wanted to talk to you about *my* article."

Sloan's large forehead wrinkled in concern. "What article is that, Miss Myrtle? You mean the next tip column? You know, I had a great idea about that article. You could do a sort of themed helpful hint column, if you're starting to run out of ideas. Like—well, one could be car care. Tips for keeping your car in smooth driving condition."

Myrtle gave him a wry look. "Right. The perfect article for me to write. A retired schoolteacher with no car."

"Okay, well, you could choose another theme. Like food. Tips for buying produce or whatnot. That type of thing." Little beads of perspiration were now forming on his forehead and he took out a wrinkled handkerchief and impatiently scrubbed them away.

"I appreciate your concern about my helpful hints column. But I wasn't referring to that at all."

"You weren't?" Sloan clutched his hands together. "Were you perhaps referring to your involvement in your friend's horoscope?"

"I wasn't. I was referring to the article I'm writing about Nandina Marshall's murder. You see, *that's* an article that I'm qualified to write," said Myrtle.

"Oh, Miss Myrtle. I just don't know." Sloan was one step away from wringing his clutched hands now. "After last time, I don't know if it's a good idea to mix you with crime fighting. Besides, you'll have your hands full with the column and with fixing that horoscope for Wanda the Wonderful or whatever we're calling her."

"I never said a word about *crime fighting*, Sloan. I merely mentioned that I'm writing an article. I'm using the pen, not the sword. It's mightier. Besides, I know a lot about this particular case. I was in the audience when the murder occurred, so I can even add firsthand knowledge to the story. Make it a more personal account."

Sloan said quickly, "You see, after the *last* time and what happened then, I sort of promised Red that I'd make sure you didn't have any more crime story assignments. Considering you were in danger and all of that."

Myrtle gave him a stern look. "For heaven's sake. I wasn't in any more danger than I am in a thousand other activities. I'm an octogenarian. Half the doctors in this country would say that even going out to get my newspaper poses a risk. Not to mention the treachery of taking a shower. If we listened to Red, I'd spend my day inside and wrapped up in cotton batting. I've no intention of living my life that way, and Red has no right to expect it. Besides, it's a free press! I'm free to write my story; you're free to publish it."

Sloan's features were even more anxious instead of relieved at Myrtle's stance. "I suppose I could always explain to Red later that you're a rogue reporter. That I didn't give you the assignment at all. That you actually just jumped in and decided to write the story yourself."

"A rogue reporter," said Myrtle with a slight smile. "I think I like that. Let's get this straight then. You *didn't* assign me the story. But when I hand you the well-written, error-free and well-researched piece that you're accustomed to from me, you'll run it. And you're not assigning the story to anyone else."

"Not that there's anyone else to assign it to," said Sloan glumly. "Our staff has been reduced to me and Mrs. Frozzle."

"You know that's not true. I just brought in Wanda the Wonderful. It's just that the *Bradley Bugle* has a lot of columns and not as many regular articles. But that's what makes people want to *read* the newspaper! It's just that a major story like this one *does* need to be covered and I happen to be the best candidate because I was there. Otherwise, people in Bradley are perfectly content reading about where Jane Parsons traveled over the summer or how many ribbons Robert Meadows collected for his heirloom tomatoes at the state fair."

Sloan looked a bit perkier at this. "You're right. All right, Miss Myrtle, we have a deal. Just protect me from Red's wrath, please. If he asks you if I had anything to do with this story, you tell him no."

"With pleasure," said Myrtle with a sniff. "I always enjoy telling Red no."

CHAPTER NINE

IMPECCABLY ON TIME, Miles rang Myrtle's doorbell at four o'clock. He still looked perky from his excellent night's sleep. Myrtle was starting to drag a little, which annoyed her. She covered her annoyance by briskly getting ready to head out for the theater.

"Miles, would you take the bag of squash, please? Should we divide it up into several plastic grocery bags instead of having it in the one bag?"

"If you're trying for the appearance of having even more squash than we do," said Miles glumly.

"I was thinking it would be easier for the cast to divide up that way," said Myrtle. She distributed the squash evenly, grabbed her purse and cane, and headed for the door.

As they pulled up to the theater, Myrtle leaned forward in the front seat. "Look! Perfect timing. There's Roscoe now."

Miles grunted. "I'd already spotted him. I may have to anonymously present him with a nice razor set."

"I'm sure there must be some people who find that scruffy look appealing. Probably most of the women in the audience," said Myrtle. "But try not to give him such a disapproving expression while we're asking him questions. We don't want him to think that we believe him to be the murderer, and that's what your expression is saying—that we disapprove of him."

"If I thought he was a murderer, I'd be looking more than disapproving at him," said Miles. "Although he does seem like a likely prospect, doesn't he? He is reported to have had an argument with the victim. He is supposed to have been romantically involved with the victim. And, having been part of the production, he certainly had the opportunity to kill Nandina."

Myrtle said impatiently, "Probably. But hurry, Miles! He looks speedy and I don't want him popping inside the theater until we can talk to him!"

Miles quickly pulled into a parking place. As soon as he had put the car into park, Myrtle was opening the door and getting out. "Roscoe? Roscoe Ragsdale?" called Myrtle.

Roscoe turned around with a slight frown. Since he hadn't grown up in the town, he didn't know Myrtle and stood there quizzically as she hurried up.

"Hi," said Myrtle a bit breathlessly. She decided to give up on the subtle approach with Roscoe since he seemed to be in a hurry. "I'm Myrtle Clover. I work for the *Bradley Bugle* and am writing a piece about the tragic death of Nandina." She hoped mentioning Nandina might work better with Roscoe. If she admitted straightaway that she was writing an investigative piece, she might scare him away. "I also wanted to offer my personal condolences. I hope you will take some home grown squash. I'll be giving some to other cast members, too."

She saw Roscoe relax a little bit and even push some dark hair off of his forehead. It occurred to Myrtle that perhaps he was thinking it would be a photo op. These show business people usually *courted* the press. Myrtle turned around to see Miles catching up with them. He was brushing a bit of invisible lint off his snowy white button-down shirt. "Miles," called Myrtle. "Are you ready to take the pictures for the piece?"

Miles looked startled, but covered it as quickly as he could. He patted his pants pockets until he located his phone. Then he pulled it out, fiddling with the device until he was able to find the camera application. Miles was not the type of person to take selfies or pictures of any kind and it was likely the very first time he'd ever used the camera at all. He looked proud of himself once he had it ready and gave Myrtle a thumbs-up.

Roscoe gave Myrtle an uncertain look. "Never mind the photographer," she said under her breath. "He's new on the staff. But he's a natural."

She started out asking Roscoe some soft questions to get him warmed up. "When did you first meet Nandina? What types of roles have you played with her in the past? What was your favorite moment with her?" Then she finally moved into, "The terrible night she was killed ...you were nearby. Did you see or hear anything unusual that night?"

Myrtle was ready for Roscoe to back away or try to give them an excuse and take off for the safety of the theater. But when Miles elaborately held up the camera at an interesting angle in order to get an artsy shot, he stayed put and looked studiously contemplative instead. That was, thought Myrtle, the very look he was going for. He was an actor through and through. She got the feeling that he was playing a part: the part of the bemused coworker.

He spread out his carefully manicured hands, "It was such a disturbing evening. Of course, I was totally in character. I tend to immerse in my parts."

Miles's mouth twisted. "As I recall, your character was the villain. It *was* early in the play, but there was a distinctly villainous air about you."

Roscoe beamed at him. "Excellent! So it was working. I love getting validation that my methods are working."

Miles wasn't sure what to say in response to this, so he started snapping pictures again. Myrtle was certain she couldn't provide any compliments on his performance, since she'd felt he'd sorely overacted. Instead, she said in a sharper tone than she'd intended, "Since you were already in the role of villain, are you sure you didn't take it a step further?"

Now Roscoe looked deflated. He gave Myrtle a reproachful glance. "Why would I have done that? I had nothing but respect for Nandina." He looked away as he said it, though.

Myrtle raised her eyebrows. "That's not what I've heard. In fact, I have a witness who saw you arguing with Nandina shortly before her death."

Roscoe looked away. "When you have two professionals who care passionately about their acting, some creative differences are bound to happen."

Miles said, "Creative differences? You're sure that's all it was?"

"What *kind* of creative differences?" asked Myrtle.

Again, that telling sideways glance that made Myrtle think he wasn't telling the truth. "Oh, you know. I thought Nandina's character needed to be more subdued in one scene. She disagreed and thought the character needed to remain sort of over the top."

Myrtle changed tack since he clearly wasn't going to be forthcoming on the argument. "Did you see anything at all during the scene change when Nandina was murdered?"

Roscoe struck a pensive pose. Obligingly, Miles snapped a picture. "It was incredibly dark back there. The cast could barely see what we were doing. I was very busy with moving the fireplace out—you know—from the previous scene. But I did think that I noticed Veronica lingering near the bed where Nandina was lying."

"Did Veronica and Nandina get on?" asked Myrtle.

Roscoe broke his pensive pose to give a great barking laugh. "Oh no," he finally managed, gasping. "Not those two. No."

"Creative differences?" asked Miles wryly.

"Or perhaps a bit more than that. Jealousy on Veronica's part. She and Nandina were always sniping at each other," said Roscoe with a shrug. His handsome features were starting to look bored.

Myrtle said, "Nandina's drink had apparently been tampered with backstage. I suppose you didn't see anything?"

"Not a thing. Except, of course, Nandina drinking. She had habits—bad habits for such a young woman. She felt that drinking before her performances relaxed her and actually helped her perform better."

Myrtle said, "And did it?"

Roscoe's mouth tightened. "It didn't. And recently, the drinking had gotten worse. She was getting sloppy with it. In fact, when Skip couldn't wake Nandina up on stage, I figured it was because she passed out. It would have been very easy for someone to have slipped sleeping pills in her drink. We all knew she would have at least one glass before a performance. And it's chaotic backstage before a performance."

Myrtle changed course. "I was returning a book at the library last night, and I had the chance to speak with your delightful wife."

Roscoe looked doubtful as to the delightful qualities his wife possessed. "You spoke with Josie about books? Or about ...this?" He gestured vaguely at the theater.

"A little of both, I guess. She was saying that she couldn't offer an opinion on what happened on opening night because she wasn't there," said Myrtle.

Roscoe cleared his throat. "That's right. Josie isn't as much of a fan of the theater. She's only occasionally in attendance."

"Although someone did spot her at the theater on opening night," continued Myrtle smoothly.

Roscoe's eyes opened wide in surprise. He said hurriedly, "They must be mistaken. Josie wasn't in the audience the other night."

Miles said, "It sounds like she was *outside* the theater. Or maybe backstage."

"Is there any reason why Josie might want to harm Nandina?" asked Myrtle.

Roscoe shook his head. "You're barking up the wrong tree if you think Josie had anything to do with this."

A car door closed behind them and Myrtle and Miles turned to look. Skip saw them, spotted the fact that they appeared to have a container of some sort with them, and quickly hurried away, pretending he hadn't seen them.

"Casserole was *that* bad, was it?" muttered Miles.

Myrtle shot him an irritated look. "If we're barking up the wrong tree, which tree *should* we be barking up?"

But Roscoe was already turning away.

Myrtle said quickly, "If you think of anything you may have forgotten, you can call me at any time. *Any* time. I rarely sleep."

"She walks the streets all night," said Miles with a devilish grin.

Roscoe barely seemed to be listening, however. "I've got to go," he said quickly.

Miles glanced down at the bag and said in a panicky voice, "Wait! Roscoe! You forgot your squash!"

"So that takes care of talking to Roscoe," said Miles. "I'm getting the feeling that we're not going to have much luck getting in touch with anyone else until after the practice. Even if we *did* get the chance, it would have to be short because they'd be running late. So what now?"

"Now we wait," said Myrtle. "We still need to talk to Veronica. I'm sure we can catch her after the practice."

"Wait? In the car? The practice could take a while, you know. Won't we get stiff?" Miles looked apprehensively at the car.

"I doubt the practice will take *that* long," said Myrtle. "And I want to make sure we're around when it lets out."

Miles unlocked the Volvo. "I should have thought ahead. I could have put a crossword puzzle book in the car. Or my book."

Myrtle nodded. "Or food. I'll admit I didn't think that part though well. We could have enjoyed a tailgate party."

"Oh, don't say that. Tailgating makes me think of burgers and hot dogs."

"And nachos and barbeque," agreed Myrtle. "Miles! Are you telling me that junk food actually sounds appealing to you right now? Will wonders never cease!"

"Not that it does me any good. I'm going to be hanging out in a theater parking lot for the next hour," said Miles glumly.

"No, we need to take advantage of this rare craving of yours. I need to prove to you that Bo's Diner does *really, really* good junk food. Here," said Myrtle, digging in her large pocketbook, "it's my treat. I insist. Go get some diner food but don't ask for it to be served healthily. Get it dripping with chili and cheese and it will positively amaze you."

"It may amaze my stomach," said Miles. "And that's not usually a good thing."

"Your stomach will survive the surprise. I'm sure of it."

Miles said, "Aren't you coming with me?" as Myrtle backed away from the Volvo.

"No, I need to stay here in case practice ends early. You go ahead," said Myrtle, waving him on.

"I can't leave you in a deserted parking lot downtown!" protested Miles.

"Why ever not? It's not as if I can be robbed. I just gave you all of my money. Unless they want a really large, beige pocketbook with multitudinous pockets filled with tissues, spare change, and half-used lipsticks. Actually, I think it will make an excellent weapon if I need one.

Miles hesitated.

"Oh, go on! And bring me back a pimento cheese dog with chili cheese fries," said Myrtle.

Miles winced and headed slowly to the car.

After he left, Myrtle heard another car approach. It was a police cruiser. Myrtle sighed. Typical. The one time she was loitering in a parking lot.

Sure enough, Red spotted her. It was almost as if he had radar out on his mother. Either that or he'd been planning on dropping by the theater himself. He pulled in quickly to a space and hopped out of the cruiser.

"Mama? It's getting late. What are you doing out here in the parking lot?" His freckled face crinkled in a frown.

"Oh, you know. I was trying to unload some squash and decided to hand them out to some of the cast members. As a kind of consolation gift," said Myrtle with a shrug.

"Squash? How'd you come about squash? You only grew tomatoes this year in your garden, didn't you?" asked Red.

"Wanda. Wanda and Crazy Dan are having some sort of miraculous squash harvest. She keeps bringing Miles squash to pay him back," said Myrtle.

"Pay him back—for *what*? What did Miles ever do to Wanda?"

"No, no, I mean pay him back in a *good* way. Because he's always giving her money."

"Funny way to pay someone back," muttered Red.

"As a matter of fact, there's great likelihood that Miles will come into even more squash soon. I don't think Wanda is going to give up ... she seemed very determined. How about if I bring any additional squash loads to your house?" asked Myrtle.

"Oh no. No, I'm allergic to squash," said Red, holding up his hands.

"Allergic to *squash*? No one's allergic to squash. And I'm pretty sure that you ate plenty of squash as a baby," said Myrtle.

"No wonder I turned out the way I did. Besides, we can develop allergies over the years. I'm positive that I did. And before you ask, Elaine and Jack are allergic, too."

Myrtle made a face. "Y'all are no fun."

Red looked around them. "So, where *is* this squash that you were trying to unload?"

"I've already given it away. Roscoe Ragsdale was the lucky recipient. And he did look pleased," said Myrtle, stubbornly.

Red said, "So why are you still skulking around the parking lot?"

"I wouldn't say I was *skulking*! I'm just waiting for Miles. He left to pick us up some supper from Bo's," said Myrtle.

"That's not like Miles to dump you at the theater and take off," said Red with a frown.

"I made him. I told him to go and I'd take in the ambiance of the theater building," said Myrtle

"You're not trying to investigate this case, are you?" Red's eyes were suspicious.

"Of course not. But I *am* writing a story on the theater. A little background on the building and what it's represented to the community over the years," said Myrtle.

Red's shoulders relaxed. "Oh, I see. A puff piece?"

This raised Myrtle's hackles, but she gritted her teeth into a smile with an effort. "That's right." And it just so happened that it was also the scene of a murder.

She added briskly, "Besides, taking in the ambiance, I thought I'd get a few quotes from Mr. Toucan. Were you going inside?"

Red shook his head. "I thought I would, but I've got a meeting with Lieutenant Perkins from the state police. We're going over our leads." He headed back to his cruiser and called over his shoulder, "You know, if you're wanting to interview someone about the theater's place in the community, you should talk to Elaine. She could probably give you a couple of quotes, considering how much time she spends over there."

"I'll have to do that, thanks." Besides, Elaine might also have some opinions over whether there was any validity to Josie's fears that her husband was having an affair with Nandina. She waved to Red as he drove off. She was glad that she'd thought of Mr. Toucan. Even though he was just the owner of the theater and didn't actually do any acting, he might still know something valuable.

Myrtle walked around the front of the building and went in through the front door to find the theater owner. The lighting was dim inside and it took a moment for her eyes to adjust. By the time she had, she already heard a gruff voice saying in surprise, "Miss Myrtle? You know we don't have any performances right now, don't you?"

Her eyes finally adjusted to the dimness of the room and she saw Mr. Toucan sitting behind the ticket box at a messy desk. He was a large awkward man with orange hair and mustache, wearing an olive tie over a dingy, khaki, button—down shirt sporting a pocket protector with only one pen in it. His eyes, behind a pair of large spectacles, had the quality of always appearing startled. Unfortunately, this was standard attire for Mr. Toucan and not a costume. Although Myrtle knew Mr. Toucan had a wistful longing to be on the stage, it was perhaps best for some people to remain patrons of the arts instead of actors themselves.

Myrtle didn't have a chance to answer his previous question before he'd already anxiously launched into another: "Are you here about a refund? I did see you on opening night, didn't I?" His large eyes appeared even more anxious behind his thick glasses."

Myrtle said, "I was here. Poor lamb," she clucked.

Mr. Toucan automatically nodded, but he seemed unsure about Nandina qualifying for lamb status. "I do have a refund policy." He started rummaging around somewhat frantically in his stacks of messy papers until he found one at the bottom of a large stack and pushed it across the ticket box counter for her to see. "It does mention no refunds in the case of acts of God."

Myrtle raised her eyebrows at this. "Acts of God? Is that what Nandina's death is? God has better, kinder things to do than strike down young women in their prime, don't you think? No, this was an act of *man*. And I believe the police do, too."

Mr. Toucan looked sadly at his refund policy paper. "I think it was an act of man, too." He cleared his throat and looked as businesslike as he could pull off. "We *are* planning an extra performance of this play for everyone who attended on opening night."

Myrtle said, "That's very nice of you. Although I'm not concerned over refunds or getting my money's worth." Particularly since she hadn't paid a dime for the tickets. "I'm here on behalf of the paper. You knew that I write for them, didn't you?"

Mr. Toucan nodded. He looked cautiously optimistic. "What kind of coverage are you going to give the theater? They say there's no such thing as bad publicity."

Myrtle smiled. Mr. Toucan hadn't even asked what *type* of article she was writing for the paper. He'd immediately assumed she was writing about the murder. It was nice to be taken seriously as a reporter. "I'll be as sympathetic toward the theater as I can. Maybe I can work in a plug for the theater being vital to the community—something like that. I know how important it is to you."

"It was my lifelong dream to own a theater," he said, looking around at the building with pride. "You know I owned the pet shop for decades here."

"It must have been hard to leave something very safe and follow your dream," said Myrtle.

He blinked at her behind the large glasses. "On the contrary, it was very easy. When you have a dream like that one, it's an imperative."

"When I was here the other night, I could tell that you'd really put some money into the place," said Myrtle. Which was true. The building had been in a horrible state when Mr. Toucan bought it. Although it wasn't in wonderful shape now, it was still much better than it was. It had been at the point of having the city consider condemning it and knocking it down. That had been, most likely, the greatest impetus for the timing of Mr. Toucan's purchase.

He heaved a great sigh. "Yes, I've put a lot of money into the building. I *had* to. Sometimes you can't really know at the beginning of a project how much everything will end up costing. You think electrical or air conditioning upgrades will cost one thing, but once you go into the wiring and walls and so forth, it ends up costing a lot more. On top of that, to draw people in during the past year and a half, I paid royalty fees to put on the big-name plays and musicals—stuff that people would pay money to see." He sighed once again. "Now I'm pretty tapped out."

"Which is why you're trying to adhere to your refund policy," said Myrtle.

He shrugged. "That money from opening night has already really been spoken for. Toward my utilities."

"Did you have a good vantage point to see what happened backstage on opening night?" asked Myrtle.

Mr. Toucan shook his head. "Sadly, no. Red has already asked me that. Sometimes I do go backstage after I've finished at the ticket office. I love to see the backstage bustle and the cast pulling everything together into a great performance. But I didn't do it much this time. I didn't even really have a chance to say goodbye to Nandina because I was so tied up in the office before the performance. I just had enough time to get to the front of the theater to introduce the play. And then I ran backstage again after ... you know." His big eyes welled up.

Myrtle was alarmed. The last thing she wanted was to be put in the position of comforting Mr. Toucan, so she continued briskly, "You didn't *see* anything, but you must have some opinions on who could have done such a thing."

Mr. Toucan hesitated.

Myrtle said, "The sooner we get this cleared up, the sooner that people will start thinking of the theater as a safe place to go again."

"That's true," said Mr. Toucan. "Now everyone thinks that someone in the cast is a killer."

"Someone in the cast *is* a killer," said Myrtle. "Unless you know of someone who might have sneaked in from the outside unnoticed. It would have to be someone very familiar with the theater's layout, though. Would Josie Ragsdale?"

Myrtle watched carefully for a response. Mr. Toucan showed surprise and then relieved. She should have known he'd latch onto any suspect who wasn't part of the cast. It would make it easier for him, PR-wise.

He said slowly, "Well, Josie would fit that bill. Yes indeedy. She has been associated with the theater for years through Roscoe."

"But, to be fair, I heard that Josie didn't really enjoy watching plays and just sort of put up with Roscoe and his acting. So would she be all that familiar with the building? Would she be able to fit in backstage?" asked Myrtle.

"She's familiar enough. Josie is at the theater fairly often, as a matter of fact. I won't argue that most of the times that she's here, she's trying to drag Roscoe back home. But that entails going backstage. Yes, she's familiar with the building." Mr. Toucan beamed at Myrtle.

"Although what would she have against Nandina?"

Mr. Toucan shifted uncomfortably. "That's all hearsay, you know. I'm a bit uneasy about passing along hearsay. I'll just say that Josie believed that Roscoe might have been involved with Nandina. Whether it's actually true or not, I have no idea. Josie isn't the kind of person to take kindly to that sort of thing. You see, she has been financing Roscoe's dream of acting. She has a lot of money and Roscoe was very keen on spending his days memorizing his lines and practicing them and not having a regular job. Josie would have been pretty angry if she'd been financing an affair along with everything else."

Myrtle said, "I know you introduced the play night before last. Doesn't the director usually do that?"

"Yes. But our director abruptly moved away from Bradley over a week ago. Family reasons of some sort. So he would be no use at all to talk to. Fortunately, this is a mature cast and they were able to direct themselves to a certain degree. And Blaine helped out quite a bit since he's such a veteran. I stepped in to speak to the audience and that sort of thing," said Mr. Toucan.

"What about others in the cast? Were any of them as unhappy with Nandina?" asked Myrtle.

Mr. Toucan absently pushed papers around on the desk, and in the process, making them even messier than they were before. "Just the type of petty things you'd expect in a small group. Nothing that anyone would murder over." He made a face at the word *murder* as if it left a sour taste in his mouth. "These people have artistic souls. They're not thugs. Veronica has taken roles in theaters all over the country with the Actor's Equity. She's a real pro, and responsible, to boot. She spends her free time at the theater helping us with sets. Besides acting, Blaine likes nothing better than penning poetry and looking out at the lake. He writes scripts at the theater when no one is here. Do these people sound like ruthless killers to you?"

Myrtle studied him. He certainly could get agitated fast. In a calming voice she said, "Of course they don't. But we can't know what's in their hearts, can we? Especially since they're actors. They're experts at playing a part. And, as I mentioned, the faster we clear this business up, the faster things can return to normal for you and the theater." She paused. "You might think to call Tippy Chambers. I'm in book club with her. The woman loves a good cause and she thinks of herself as a patron of the arts, although her taste in fiction runs to beach books. You might ask her if she'd be interested in forming a *Friends of the Theater* foundation or something."

Mr. Toucan nodded, looking thoughtful. "Of course, of course, Miss Myrtle. And I appreciate it, I really do." Although he seemed a little conflicted on that point.

A MINUTE AFTER MYRTLE returned to her parking lot vigil, Miles pulled up. She climbed into his car, which was filled with the aroma of French fries and grease.

"Ahh," she said appreciatively. "Let's dig in."

Miles carefully spread napkins over his lap and handed a bunch to Myrtle. "It's a good thing I store a bottle of antacid in my car," he mumbled. He handed Myrtle her order and then gingerly pulled out a hot dog for himself. "Was it quiet here the whole time?"

"No. As a matter of fact, it wasn't quiet at all. Red drove up to harass me. And he was surprised and disturbed by the fact that you left me in a parking lot downtown," said Myrtle with an annoyed sigh.

Miles raised his eyebrows in alarm. "I hope you told him it wasn't my idea." He looked uncomfortable. "I hate the thought that Red thinks I wasn't behaving like a gentleman."

"Why *would* you behave like a gentleman? We're not dating, we're friends. And I'm perfectly capable of looking after myself. I carry a weapon with me at all times," said Myrtle, giving her cane a nudge with her knee. "Anyway, I calmed him down. At least, I calmed him down over that point and then he got all fired up that I was at the theater to investigate."

"So I suppose you were able to come up with a story for why you're here?" Miles took a tentative bite of his hot dog. Then he looked surprised and took another bite. "This is pretty good," he admitted.

"I told him that I was doing a story for the paper on the theater and its role in the community through the years. Something boring like that," said Myrtle. "Then, to back up my story, I went in to talk to Mr. Toucan."

"Ah. So you killed two birds with one stone," said Miles. "What did he have to say?" He took a very large bite of his hot dog this time.

"He groused a lot," said Myrtle. "He was concerned about the bottom line for the theater. To be fair, though, he did seem to have a lot going on. His renovation work ran into snags, his director moved away from town, and then he had a murder on opening night. He had the right to grouse."

"Did he have any information on Nandina's death? See anything? Know of any gossip?" asked Miles. He reached into the greasy paper bag for another hot dog.

"He said he was really busy that night so he didn't spend as much time with the cast. He corroborated that Josie believed Roscoe was having an affair with Nandina. Other than that, he spent his time defending his cast. He doesn't seem to want anyone to think he's got a murderer in the theater. As I said, he was thinking about his bottom line. It seems he is low on funds."

Miles said, "If things continue down this path, he'll be short on cast members, too."

They sat there in the car for a few minutes, eating their meal, drinking sweet tea, and thinking about the murder.

Then Miles said, "Have any French fries you're not planning on eating?"

CHAPTER TEN

IT TOOK A BIT LONGER for Veronica to surface than they'd planned—long enough that, after her large meal, Myrtle was beginning to feel drowsy.

When the back door to the theater opened, though, Myrtle was suddenly wide awake. Veronica came out of the doorway, smirking as she said something light to Roscoe, who was grinning back at her. She pushed a hand through her long, strawberry-blonde hair and it swished across her shoulders.

Myrtle said to Miles, "They seem very friendly, too. Do you think that maybe Josie was mistaken and Roscoe was actually having an affair with Veronica?"

Miles hiccupped. "Excuse me," he said with a sigh. He fumbled in his center console for his antacid. "Finishing off your chili cheese fries was a mistake."

"I'm going to stop speculating and just go ahead and talk with her. This cast is so intertwined that I can't tell a couple from a couple of friends," grumbled Myrtle.

"We'd better hurry," said Miles. "Looks like she parked pretty far away from us."

Myrtle leaped out of the Volvo and tore off through the parking lot, cane thumping furiously as she went. Miles hurried to keep up with her, hitting his key fob to lock his door.

"Veronica!" sang out Myrtle. "Veronica?"

"Lucky thing that Roscoe has already gotten in his car. He might find all these conversations a little suspicious," said Miles darkly. He gave another hiccup as they gained speed to try to catch Veronica before she got into her car.

"Veronica!" hollered Myrtle. Then, under her breath and panting a bit said, "Is the woman deaf?"

Finally, Veronica turned around. She gave them a doubtful look. "Sorry. Do I know you?"

"Most likely not," said Miles.

"We're with the newspaper," said Myrtle. "At least I am. Miles is sort of a ... cub reporter."

Miles shot her a dark look.

Myrtle quickly corrected herself. "Actually, it would be more accurate to call Miles a budding photojournalist."

He seemed somewhat more pleased by this description.

Veronica looked blankly at Myrtle. "The paper? I thought Sloan was with the paper."

"Exactly. Sloan is my editor," said Myrtle. "I'm doing a story for the paper on the theater." She pulled out a small notebook and a pencil from her large pocketbook as she hung her cane on her arm.

A distasteful look crossed Veronica's freckled face at the mention of the newspaper and Myrtle hastily seized on the excuse she'd given Red. "It's not on the tragic events of the other night. It's more of a profile of the theater and its place in the community. I'd love to get some quotes from you."

Myrtle could hear Miles sigh again. He was clearly sorry that they were going to have to take a convoluted route to get any information. He obligingly took out his phone and aimed it at Veronica.

The transformation in Veronica's attitude was amazing. She started smiling alluringly at Miles's camera. Miles responded by fumbling the camera and nearly dropping it.

Myrtle ignored him and set about asking a few easy questions about what Veronica thought about the theater, fond memories, etc. Miles continued snapping pictures.

The interview progressed until Myrtle found a good point for a transition question. "Since this tragedy has the potential for creating a real drop-off in traffic for the theater, do you have any words to help persuade theater goers to attend this performance?"

Veronica rolled her eyes, "I think it will be packed. Totally packed. People are so morbid, you know. They'll be there to gape at the murder scene even if they don't care a thing about the play we're in."

Myrtle asked, "It's hard to think of that lovely theater as the scene of a murder. Tragic. Any ideas what might have happened the other night? Did you see anything or hear anything?"

Veronica's expression said that she thought Myrtle was being morbidly curious herself. "The lights were very dim and the scene transition music was playing too loudly. My ears were ringing. Besides, it wasn't as though Nandina was screaming for help. I doubt she even made a sound at all. Everyone knew she drank before performances. She was probably half asleep when it happened."

"Can you imagine who might have done such a thing?" asked Miles without hiccupping once.

Veronica said, "Oh, everyone wanted to strangle Nandina." She flushed, her normally-porcelain skin now nearly the same shade as her auburn hair, realizing that she'd made a poor choice of words. "I mean, Nandina had a habit of getting on people's nerves."

"Like who, in particular?" pressed Myrtle. Miles hiccupped again with a sigh and Myrtle gave him a severe look, dropping her tiny notebook into her pocketbook as she rummaged for a small water bottle for Miles. Like Mary Poppins, Myrtle had nearly *everything* in her bag.

"Well, Roscoe, for one. He and Nandina had something going on. I spend a lot of time at the theater between making sets and practicing my lines. I just love the place." She paused and looked expectantly at Myrtle. "You can quote me on that."

Myrtle grabbed her notebook and pen again and made a big pretense of taking notes. She prompted Veronica, "You've seen Roscoe and Nandina together while you've been at the theater?"

"I certainly have. Not in a passionate clinch or anything. But they were definitely trying not to be seen. There was something going on, for sure."

"Anybody else?" asked Myrtle.

Veronica tilted her head to the side and gave Myrtle a suspicious look. "What does all this have to do with the theater's place in the community?"

Myrtle ignored her question and continued, "It's been suggested that you might have had issues with Nandina, too. That maybe Roscoe wasn't the only one arguing with her."

A petulant expression crossed Veronica's face. "*Everyone* had issues with Nandina. Larger ones than I did. My issues were minor quibbles."

Miles, now thankfully hiccup-free, said, "Even Skip? Did Skip have issues with Nandina?"

Veronica said darkly, "Skip had the most issues of anybody. They were just *different* issues. He had a very unhealthy, unnatural obsession with Nandina."

Her expression suggested that Veronica was piqued that he didn't have an obsession with *her.*

Myrtle said, "It wasn't merely a crush?"

"Absolutely not. He was stalking her. There, I've said it. I'll say the same to the police if they ask me. I overheard Nandina telling Cady that she spotted Skip in the bushes outside her apartment. He was spying on her." Veronica shook her head. "If you ask me, he's the one with all the issues."

Miles said, "But if he loved her so much, why would he have killed her?"

"Why not?" asked Veronica archly. "Perhaps he got tired of waiting for her to discover him. Perhaps he was jealous of her relationship with Roscoe. And I never said he *loved* her. I said he was obsessed with her. Those are two different things."

They were indeed.

Myrtle asked, "What about Roscoe's wife, Josie?"

Veronica snorted. "The little librarian? Why she even bothers to work, I don't know. She certainly doesn't *have* to work.

But to answer your question, she *could* have done it. She didn't just have issues with Nandina, she *hated* her."

"Because she thought Roscoe was involved with Nandina," said Myrtle.

Veronica's brown eyes were suspicious again. "You're not quoting me on this, are you? I only want to be quoted when I'm talking about the theater."

Myrtle stuffed the little notebook back in her purse. "You're off the record."

"Josie was constantly lurking around the theater, hoping to catch Nandina and Roscoe together. She knew the theater like the back of her hand. She could have stolen up the back stairs," Veronica gestured to the steep steps leading up to the back of the theater, "slipped backstage, murdered Nandina, and left before anyone knew she was there."

"Are there any security cameras or anything? That you've noticed, anyway?" asked Miles.

Veronica leveled her gaze at him. "Are you kidding me? If Toucan had that kind of money, I wouldn't have to be going back tonight to repair set pieces."

Myrtle nodded. "What about Blaine? I haven't heard you say anything about him."

Veronica shrugged. "Not a lot to tell. He was like the rest of us—if Nandina got on his nerves, he snapped at her. Other than that, they were pretty good." She changed gears suddenly and asked, "Why aren't you asking any questions about Cady? She could have done it, you know."

Myrtle said, "No, actually, she couldn't have done it. She had car trouble and her ride didn't drop her off until after the curtain went up."

Veronica shrugged again. "Maybe. That's the way she tells it, anyway."

"Did Cady have something against Nandina?"

"Oh, I don't know. Nandina probably just got on her nerves like the rest of us. I think, in some ways, she was impressed by her, you know? Because Nandina was ... pretty." Veronica acted as if it pained her to admit it.

Miles said kindly, "I think Cady must have looked up to you, too. Considering all your theater experience."

Veronica made a face. It was clear that she'd rather be admired for her beauty than her experience.

"Maybe. And now I think I should get going. Good luck with the story." And she quickly got in her car and left.

They were quiet as Miles drove Myrtle home. When they pulled up in Myrtle's driveway, he said, "Now don't stew all night over this. It won't do any good."

"I just feel as if there's something I'm *missing*. Some sort of clue I should be picking up on," said Myrtle.

"Well, I didn't pick up on it either, so don't worry. There's probably nothing there."

MYRTLE TRIED TO TAKE Miles's words to heart. She pushed the investigation out of her mind as she opened a can of cat food for Pasha and mindlessly stroked her. She thought about other things as she read her book before bed. And she tried with great fervor to put it all out of her head as she tossed around in her bed, trying to sleep. Nothing seemed to work. Finally, around four a.m., she gave up, got dressed, and made the coffee. She was pleasantly surprised to see the newspaper had come.

An hour later she'd finished the crossword, drunk a large cup of coffee, and was cooking breakfast. Myrtle was scrambling some eggs and frying some bacon when the phone rang. This made her blink. Doorbell rings before dawn? Knocks on her door? She was used to that. A ringing phone was something else entirely.

She hurried to the phone and picked up. "Hello?" she breathlessly demanded. "Hello!"

"Myrtle, it's Elaine."

Now Myrtle was very concerned, indeed. Elaine simply didn't call her at five in the morning. For one thing, she was very focused on dealing with a just-awakened Jack. This involvement included doling out Cheerios and other foods to her preschool son. She was very Jack-centric at five o'clock a.m. And it was worrying that she was on the phone at all.

"Is Jack okay?" asked Myrtle, clutching her stomach as it churned.

"Oh! Yes, Myrtle, Jack is great. Better than great—he's still asleep."

Waves of relief swept over Myrtle. Then she thought a second and said, "Red's okay isn't he?" Somehow she felt less-worried about Red. It wasn't that she didn't love him to pieces. It was just that Red was so very capable of taking care of himself. It was so difficult to imagine a scenario where he could be in trouble.

"No, no, Red's fine, too. I'm sorry, I'm doing a bad job of relieving your mind. It's just that I'm still so foggy and half-asleep, myself. *Everyone* is fine. Well, everyone but Roscoe Ragsdale. Because he's dead."

CHAPTER ELEVEN

"DEAD?" MYRTLE WANDERED back over to the kitchen table and plopped down in a chair.

"That's right. Red just got the call a little while ago. Veronica apparently arrived at the theater earlier to finish fixing some set issues. She saw his body crumpled at the bottom of those back stairs that lead up to the back door stage entrance," said Elaine.

Myrtle said, "And I bet he didn't fall."

"Oh, I think he *did* fall. After he was hit on the head with something very hard. At least, that's what Red seems to think. Someone whacked him with something hard on his head and then he took a tumble down the stairs," said Elaine. "Red contacted the state police to let them know and he's out working it. But I wanted to let you know and ... of course ... I knew you were up."

"Thanks, Elaine. I'm sorry to hear this, but it does make things very interesting."

Elaine sighed. "And now I'm hearing stirrings upstairs so I better go ahead and get Jack's breakfast ready. I tried to go back to sleep, but when I heard about poor Roscoe, I just couldn't do it."

Myrtle thoughtfully set the phone back on the hook. She decided she'd share this new development in the case with Miles. Surely he would be up at this hour. In the unlikely case that he wasn't, she decided to bring a peace offering with her: a coffee tumbler with the coffee made just the way Miles liked it. With her head spinning with new information and with her cane in one hand and coffee in the other, she set out down the street.

About halfway to Miles's house, she gasped as something brushed past her. She relaxed when she saw it was Pasha. "Sweet girl," she said to the black cat. "Want to walk me safely to see Miles?"

Pasha was in quite the social mood and kept making little meows as they went as if they were holding a conversation. Myrtle talked back to her. She wasn't sure that she knew what they were saying to each other, but she had the feeling that it might have something to do with food.

As she walked up Miles's walkway, she didn't see any lights on in the house. He was about to get an early-morning wakeup call. She tapped on the door and waited. Pasha waited with her, bumping her furry head against the side of Myrtle's leg.

There was no answer. She knocked harder and waited. No lights came on; no one came to the door. Finally, she rang the doorbell and a minute later a frazzled-looking Miles answered. "Something wrong?" he asked blearily. "Hey!" he added as Pasha bounded in.

Myrtle slid past him inside, handing him coffee as she went. "Nothing's wrong personally, no. But we have another body on our hands. You don't mind Pasha, do you?

Of course Miles minded Pasha. But this time he was too busy thinking about the identity of the body. Which meant Pasha could stay as long as she wanted.

Miles's eyes grew large as Myrtle plopped down on his sofa. Pasha, likely wanting to butter Myrtle up in case there was a chance at some tuna, hopped up next to her and lay her head adoringly on Myrtle's leg. "Another? Whose?" Then he raised up a hand. "Wait, let me guess." He paused a moment in thought. "Veronica?"

Myrtle said, "Why Veronica?"

"I don't know. She was sort of unpleasant. Let's just say that I wouldn't have been surprised." He rubbed his eyes and then took a large gulp from the coffee Myrtle brought.

"Well, it wasn't Veronica, unpleasant or not. It was Roscoe," said Myrtle.

Miles looked thoughtful. "He didn't seem as if he knew anything. And, if he didn't know anything, why would anyone want to kill him?"

"He seemed to be holding something back. I kept having this feeling last night that I was missing something," said Myrtle. She absently rubbed Pasha, who responded by rolling over on her back. But Myrtle knew better than to accept that invitation for a belly rub. It usually ended up badly. "Wait, you know, I think I remember what it is. Do you remember how Roscoe told us we were on the wrong track?"

"Barking up the wrong tree; wasn't that what he said?" asked Miles. Pasha glared coolly at him. Possibly because of the barking reference.

"So what if we were really focused in the wrong direction?" asked Myrtle.

"I presume we *were* focused in the wrong direction if we thought Roscoe was the killer. Unless you're saying that maybe Roscoe did kill Nandina and someone killed Roscoe for revenge," said Miles. He kept a wary eye on Pasha who was now cleaning one of her paws but still casting him reproving looks.

"Somehow, I just don't think it's that complicated. I think we got something *else* wrong. And I wonder if it was Roscoe's relationship with Nandina," said Myrtle.

"Their affair?"

"Right. Except that I don't believe there *was* an affair. Think about it—the only reason we thought that is because *Josie* thought it. And because Roscoe's wife thought it and lurked around the theater to catch Nandina and Roscoe together, *everyone* thought it was true. But what if Josie were completely wrong? After all, other accounts of Roscoe and Nandina together mention arguments. What if those weren't lover's quarrels at all?" asked Myrtle. "Do you remember in the diner the other day? It was difficult because we didn't really know the cast then. But Nandina seemed to be taunting Roscoe over giving his wife a call. It made him very agitated. If Nandina had been talking about a friendly visit to see Josie, why would he have had the same reaction?"

Miles nodded slowly. "Maybe Nandina was blackmailing Roscoe. Maybe that's why they were always trying to meet privately."

"Exactly. Because, think about it. We've heard that Josie was completely supporting Roscoe and his passion for the theater. He would be desperate not to lose that. And, considering how upset Josie was at even the unsubstantiated rumor that her husband and Nandina Marshall were a couple, she wouldn't have been likely to kept supporting him that way. She probably would have divorced him," said Myrtle.

"What would Nandina have been blackmailing Roscoe *over*, though?" asked Miles.

"An affair. Maybe Nandina knew about an indiscretion on Roscoe's part and was threatening to tell Josie about it if Roscoe didn't pay up. She was even starting to taunt him in front of other cast members. He would have had to have felt anxious and threatened over it. That would explain the arguments. After all, *Roscoe* doesn't have a ton of money, Josie does. Who knows how much cash Roscoe would have been able to put his hands on without asking Josie for it?" Myrtle waved her hands in the air and Pasha leaped up to bat at them. Since Pasha was fully armed with claws, Myrtle hastily stopped waving her hands.

Miles said, "Probably not enough money to satisfy Nandina. That sounds to me like another argument for Roscoe murdering Nandina. She wanted more money to stay quiet. He didn't have the money. They argued. She threatened him. He killed her." Pasha jumped fluidly down from Myrtle's lap and walked over to sit next to Miles on the sofa. She stared at him from inches away. He kept a careful eye on her and said, "Then maybe someone on that stage saw something. They didn't think anything of it at the time but then later realized that it implicated Roscoe. It was probably that Skip kid. The one who's so crazy over Nandina."

"Maybe," said Myrtle reluctantly. "Although I believe there are other possibilities."

"Who was Roscoe seeing then, if he weren't having an affair with Nandina?" asked Miles. "Veronica?"

Myrtle made a face. "I don't see it. I didn't see any sparks between those two at all. Not in the diner and not onstage. No obvious chemistry."

"Surely not Cady?" asked Miles. He sounded rather scandalized. "She seems much, much too young for him."

"You were just prejudiced against Roscoe because he had a beard," said Myrtle. "He wasn't all that old. And he was handsome, too. He would have worked out well on the cast of *Tomorrow's Promise.* But no, I don't really see the two of them, either. Maybe it's an outsider. I'll have to see what Red has to say about it."

"Do you really think Red is going to give you any tips?" Miles raised his eyebrows. "That sounds like exactly the type of information that Red is likely to keep under wraps."

"True. Or Elaine!" Myrtle brightened. "I could ask Elaine to see what she can find out. There's got to be some sort of gathering of the cast and volunteers to discuss Roscoe's death. I could volunteer to watch Jack for her."

"So, is that our plan for the day? Try to get the scoop from Elaine?" asked Miles. "Because, if we have a plan, I think I'm ready to try and fall back asleep. I might even be able to drop off."

"That's our plan. And, if for some reason Elaine can't get over there or the theater has a closed meeting, I guess we can start trying to interview potential suspects again. Under the pretense of the paper, for sure, since it's been so recent that we've talked to them," said Myrtle.

"If they don't run away when they see us. I think our names are now forever linked to squash for these people," said Miles with a shudder.

CHAPTER TWELVE

BACK AT HOME, MYRTLE dialed Elaine's number. "Have you heard at all from the theater? Mr. Toucan?"

Elaine, who had a children's TV show playing in the background, laughed and said, "No one calls this early in the morning, Myrtle. Only you. Anyone calling at odd hours calls Red's work phone."

Myrtle felt rather abashed. "Well, I don't call *everyone* at this hour. Only Miles, who never sleeps, and you, after I've made sure your lights were still on and that you hadn't fallen back asleep."

"It's okay, I was already up, as you knew. No hope in going back to bed with Jack around. What's going on?"

"I was thinking," said Myrtle in a very altruistic tone, "that surely the theater would be holding some sort of gathering to hash out what's happened. You know, to discuss the tragedies with the cast and the volunteers and other staff. Since you've been so closely involved with the theater, I thought I could watch Jack for you while you attended."

There was a pause on the other end of the line. Then Elaine said, "So that I can report back in?"

"Only if you *want* to. Of course, it would be most definitely appreciated if you do," said Myrtle.

"I haven't heard from anyone yet. From the theater, I mean. Of course, it's still really early."

"Not even an email? Because it seems to me that this is the sort of thing that's going to make big news," said Myrtle.

"Oh, email, right. I haven't even had a chance to check it yet today." There was a pause again and Elaine said, "You know, I *do* already have a message about Roscoe's death. And they say that anyone who is available this morning is welcome to come and talk about the tragedy at ten-thirty. They're big on talking about feelings there, so I suppose they're trying to help us process it."

"Want to bring Jack by at ten, then? With a few toys, maybe. I feel like he's getting tired of playing with the same toys at my house all the time," said Myrtle.

It was all set. And Myrtle looked at the clock to see it was not even six a.m.

Myrtle decided once again that it was most inconvenient that people got up so late in the day. There were so many different errands she could run if everyone woke as early as she did. She needed to go to the post office, for one. For another, she really couldn't go on eating the bizarre odds and ends that she'd picked up on sale at the grocery store with Red. Miles would need to be conscripted into service as her chauffeur. But the store wasn't open yet, either. No one in Bradley had apparently heard of Ben Franklin and his excellent "early to bed, early to rise" notions. It certainly was a pity.

An insistent blast of the doorbell followed by a brisk, demanding knock made Myrtle jump. Being jumpy made her irritable. "Coming!" she snapped. She supposed she must have left something at Miles's house and he'd run by to return it. It wasn't like him to scare her to death with the bell and knocking, though.

She jerked the door open and saw, to her surprise, a rather ordinary-looking brunette woman with red eyes standing on her doorstep. Myrtle blinked at her in astonishment.

The young woman looked at her levelly and said, "Myrtle Clover? You're Myrtle Clover?" Her tear-reddened eyes registered surprise as she gazed at Myrtle.

"That's right. And I've already been saved, if you're out saving people. Although I will go on the record as saying that it's awfully early in the day to go around saving folks. You should rethink your schedule," said Myrtle. She started to close the door.

The young woman put her hand out to stop the door from closing any more. "I was just surprised, that's all. At your age. You're the Myrtle Clover who works for the newspaper, is that correct? The reporter?"

Now Myrtle stepped back to allow the young woman to enter. "That's right. I'm Myrtle Clover, the reporter." She felt her ego swell just the slightest bit at the job title. "Please come in."

"I'm Winnie Granger, by the way. I apologize for the early morning visit. I've been up all night and I don't think I even realized the time until you mentioned it." Now that the young woman had come into the light a little bit, Myrtle could see that she was attractive in her own way with thick brown hair and beautiful skin. She felt a slight recognition, too, as if she were somehow acquainted with Winne. She was a bit older than Myrtle had originally thought—maybe she was in her early thirties. Perhaps the unfortunate redness of her eyes had to do with the fact that she hadn't had any sleep.

Myrtle was able to hold onto this fiction until Winnie suddenly burst into tears, immediately demonstrating the reason behind the redness. As usual, Myrtle felt at a loss before busying herself by tracking down a box of tissues, ushering Winnie to a comfortable chair, and then thrusting the tissue box at her. And waiting, making clucking/soothing noises every now and then.

Finally Winnie was able to control herself. "I'm so sorry," she said miserably. "I'm not usually an emotional person. But I've been on such a roller coaster lately." Her voice was scratchy from crying.

Myrtle cleared her own throat in response to Winnie's scratchiness. "No apologies needed. I'm guessing this has something to do with the unexpected death of Roscoe Ragsdale?" But who *was* this young woman? She hadn't seen her around the theater and didn't know her as a cast member.

Winnie nodded. "I learned about it last night. The police chief answered Roscoe's phone when I called it. I'd been trying to reach Roscoe and he hadn't picked up so I was trying again. That's when he told me."

Myrtle pursed her lips. "I hope the police chief was sensitive when he told you."

"As much as he could be. He was, understandably, curious about *me*," said Winnie. "You see, I haven't been around the theater much. I used to be very involved, but then my work added more hours onto my schedule and I haven't had the time to really participate."

"Where do you work?" asked Myrtle, still trying to figure out why Winnie looked vaguely familiar.

"At the pharmacy downtown," said Winnie.

Ah. That explained it. Being an octogenarian required a certain familiarity with the pharmacy.

"And you and Roscoe were having an affair, is that right?" asked Myrtle, trying to be delicate and look sympathetic all at once. Although that was difficult to pull off since she generally disapproved.

"That's right," said Winnie, raising her chin a little. Instead of looking abashed, she looked defiant. A woman to be reckoned with, for sure.

"And ... you're here because I'm a reporter for the *Bugle*, is that correct? How did you even know that I was assigned to the story?" asked Myrtle.

"From Roscoe. Roscoe told me you were. And he also mentioned that everyone said you didn't sleep and that you were seen walking down the street at all hours."

Myrtle bristled a little at this. "Well, I don't know if I'd have said *all hours*."

Winnie gave her a quizzical look, but nodded hastily, "At any rate, that's why I'm here. I wanted to set the record straight. I cared about Roscoe, but I never did agree with him on one thing. The secrecy. I'm the kind of person who likes everything out in the open," she said brusquely.

"And Roscoe didn't want his wife to know about your affair," said Myrtle.

Winnie pursed her lips. "It's not what you think. It isn't because he wanted to stay married to Josie and have an affair on the side."

"No?" asked Myrtle, thinking of Josie's fat bank account and Roscoe's fondness for acting instead of holding down a traditional job.

"He was waiting for a good time to tell her. It seems like Josie has had one disaster occur after another. Her dad was sick in Georgia and then Josie had some sort of stressful thing going on at work. Although in a library, I really can't imagine what that would have been." Again with the pursed, disapproving looks.

"So you're saying that Roscoe intended on leaving Josie and marrying you?"

"Of course I am," snapped Winnie. "But now?" She sobbed.

Myrtle didn't want to face a tearful Winnie again and hastily interjected, "So why see me? What does this have to do with Nandina's murder? Or doesn't it?"

"Here's the thing. There was another reason Roscoe didn't want Josie to know about our relationship. He was concerned for my safety. He thought that all the stress Josie had been under had somehow messed with her mind. She was right to suspect that Roscoe was having an affair, but she looked in the wrong direction."

Myrtle said, "Right. She thought Roscoe was interested in Nandina. She wasn't the only person who thought that, either."

Winnie snorted. "As if Roscoe could find someone like Nandina interesting. Nandina was nice to look at, but completely vacuous. Roscoe prefers intellectual companionship."

Seeing Winnie, Myrtle had no doubt this was true. "But Josie didn't realize that."

"Clearly, Josie didn't realize a lot of things. Roscoe told me that I should lie low for a little while, for my own safety. He said that Josie had confronted him with her suspicions about Nandina and he was sure that she meant to do Nandina harm. He didn't want me to be in any danger. And here we are with Nandina dead." Winnie absently pushed a hand through her hair.

"So what exactly is it that you're wanting me to do?" asked Myrtle.

"If you're doing a story about Roscoe's death, I want you to quote me," said Winnie. "Besides being *devastated* by Roscoe's murder, I'm also furious. I'm furious that I'm going to be left out of the funeral planning. I'm furious I don't have any Roscoe keepsakes to remember him by. And I'm furious that the truth of our life together is stuck in a shadowy place where I'm not allowed to grieve openly for him.

Myrtle shook her head. "I don't think it's a great idea to accuse Josie of murdering Nandina. Not in the *Bradley Bugle*. It's libel. That's what you're suggesting, isn't it?"

Winnie snorted impatiently. "We can just say that Roscoe and I were in a relationship. The readers can read between the lines."

Myrtle thought Winnie was putting a little too much faith in the reading comprehension abilities of people in Bradley. "Won't this mean that Josie will come after you? If you think that she attacked Nandina?"

Winnie smirked. "I've just become the proud owner of what is, from all accounts, a most loving and enthusiastically protective Rottweiler. I'm to pick it up from the breeder today."

"So, to recap, what I'm reporting is that Winnie Granger, a self-reported friend of Roscoe Ragsdale's, says she is devastated by his untimely death."

Winnie added, "And that I'm working closely with authorities to help put the killer behind bars."

"Make sure you lock your doors, dog or no dog," muttered Myrtle. "But let me ask you something. What if ... hear me out here ... what if Josie had nothing to do with this at all?"

"But she must have. She must have been insanely jealous of Nandina. Then she couldn't live with the constant reminder that Roscoe favored someone else and she killed Roscoe in a fit of pique." Winnie's hands tightly squeezed the tissues she was still holding.

It all reminded Myrtle of an episode of *Tomorrow's Promise* soap opera. "Right. Or not. What if Roscoe realized that he knew something about the murder? What if he took bits of information and pieced together the killer's identity? What I'm asking you, Winnie, is if Roscoe seemed troubled by something. Did he mention that anything was bothering him? Did he act differently at all?"

"As I mentioned, we weren't spending much time together since Roscoe was worried about my safety. But when he called me with that cheap pay-as-you-go cell phone that he got to talk with me on, he did seem really preoccupied. As if he was wrestling with something. And he told me, again, that he was planning on leaving Josie and marrying me. That he might be about to come into some money."

"What kind of money? An inheritance?"

Winnie shook her head. "Roscoe hadn't mentioned anyone dying. I wondered if maybe he'd found a day job."

That seemed most unlikely since Roscoe wasn't known to be someone who liked doing anything but acting. Maybe Roscoe was planning on blackmailing someone.

CHAPTER THIRTEEN

MYRTLE WAS SO ENGAGED in writing the article for the *Bradley Bugle* and in trying to give it journalistic integrity instead of letting it descend into tabloid territory, that she was startled at the knock on the door at ten o'clock.

"This place is busier than the Charlotte airport," she muttered to herself as she walked to her front door.

It all came back to her when she saw Jack's sunny face smiling up at her. He hugged her around her leg and then trotted inside.

Elaine gave her a doubtful expression. Usually when Jack came over, Myrtle had her house completely set up for the visit. She'd have cartoons on the television, a coloring book set out, a bowl of snacks on the coffee table, and a basket of toys on the floor. This time, there was only Myrtle, still wearing bedroom slippers and clutching a cup of coffee.

"We said ten, didn't we?" asked Elaine anxiously. "Are you sure this works for you today?"

"It certainly does! Jack and I are going to ... well, I think we're going to play out in the backyard. Or maybe trace our hands on paper. Or do shadow puppets. I haven't completely figured it out yet, but I thought maybe Jack could help brainstorm with me." She'd have to finish the article later. But, since Sloan technically wasn't even expecting an additional story, she had a feeling that would work out just fine. "Besides, Miles is going to drop by and entertain us." She was sure that Miles would drop by. It was the entertainment part that he wasn't actually aware of yet.

Sure enough, it was about thirty minutes later when she heard Miles tap lightly on her door. She knew it had to be Miles because everyone else pounded on her door as if she were deaf as a post. "Come in!" she hollered from the kitchen.

" 'Min!" yelled Jack, echoing her.

"Mr. Miles is going to play with us, Jack. Won't that be fun?" asked Myrtle.

Miles opened the door and peered inside. "Myrtle?"

"In the kitchen!" called Myrtle.

"Kitchen!" agreed her Greek chorus.

Miles appeared a moment later in the kitchen door. "Hi Jack! Having fun?"

Jack was standing on a tall stool in front of the kitchen sink. He beamed at Miles and struck his hand at the water in the sink, instantly covering both himself and Myrtle.

"Swimming, Myrtle?" asked Miles in an amused voice.

"Just because we're soaked doesn't mean we're swimming," said Myrtle with a sniff. "It only means that we're having a good time. Technically, we're ice fishing. Show Mr. Miles, Jack."

Jack held up a strainer. And then he beat the water in the sink with it, sending plumes of water up.

"We've put ice cubes in the sink and Jack is busily fishing them out and putting them in a bowl," said Myrtle. "Ice fishing."

"Very clever. And you are multitasking by also simultaneously bathing Jack and yourself. Ingenious." Miles grinned at her.

"I know. I'm thinking we should segue into the backyard now to dry off in the warmth of the sun. Would you like to accompany us?"

"I'd love to." Miles glanced at the kitchen counter. "It looks as if your cell phone is trying to communicate with you, Myrtle. Lights are blinking."

"Oh, that's right. It was making all kinds of racket a little while ago, but since Jack and I were playing with water, I decided it was best if my phone and I were segregated. Can you check it for me? I'm way too soggy to mess with electronics."

Myrtle held Jack's hands while he jumped from the stool to the floor. They headed out the back door. Miles followed slowly with Myrtle's phone.

"So, what did she say?" asked Myrtle, as she watched Jack try to feed a dandelion to one of her yard gnomes.

"I'm not sure I've figured out your phone yet," grunted Miles. He continued pressing buttons on the front and sides of the phone.

"Are you *sure* you were an engineer?" asked Myrtle skeptically.

"I wasn't a *computer* engineer," said Miles stiffly.

"Here," said Myrtle, wiping her hands briskly on her navy slacks, "I can check it."

Miles handed it over and Myrtle turned it on and pulled up her text messages. She squinted at the phone. "Elaine is sending me pictures from the cast meeting. I guess she wants me to draw my own conclusions from studying the suspects."

"And what do the suspects look like?" asked Miles. He took the dandelion that Jack handed him and held it absently as Jack now dodged and ran in between gnomes.

"Skip looks stressed out, like he hasn't slept in days," said Myrtle.

"Wracked with guilt?" asked Miles.

"Maybe guilt. Maybe just insomnia. Who knows? Let's see. Not a very flattering picture of Veronica. But she certainly appears smug. Like the cat who ate the canary." Myrtle held up her phone and Miles peered at it.

"A most unpleasant woman, I thought," he murmured. "Wonder what she has to be so pleased over?"

"Well, even if she *didn't* have anything to do with Nandina's death, it still benefited her tremendously. Now she can have those romantic lead parts that she liked so much. She has everything in the world to be smug over," said Myrtle.

"Did Elaine snap a picture of everyone else? And, really, shouldn't we tell Elaine to be cautious and stop taking pictures now? Surely she's making herself a target for the killer."

"Oh no, Elaine can take pictures quite surreptitiously. You'd think that she was merely checking her emails. Yes, here's a picture of Blaine." Myrtle tilted her phone and looked at it from different angles. She increased the size of the picture and reduced it again. "I can't really see anything at all from this picture. Either Elaine didn't choose a particularly telling moment to record, or else Blaine is hiding his emotions well."

"He *is* an actor, after all. He should be an expert at hiding his emotions," said Miles.

"And here's one of Cady. She looks like she's taking everything in. Which she should, because she certainly seems like the biggest gossip of the group. We need to talk to her again and see what she makes of all this. Now that we have another murder, we'll need to interview *all* our suspects again and find out where everyone was." Jack was peeking out at Myrtle from behind one of the larger gnomes and Myrtle grinned at him. "Peekaboo!"

"What else have you got?" asked Miles.

"Well, one of Mr. Toucan. He does look very upset. Red in the face and his eyes are wild and staring. He looks rather like a puffer fish. But I can't think why Elaine is taking a picture of *him*. He was in the ticket booth most of the time. He certainly wasn't up on the stage strangling Nandina," said Myrtle.

She showed the picture to Miles. "He does look vaguely suspicious."

"Not suspicious, *upset*. And why wouldn't he be? Now there's a *second* actor killed at his theater. He has every reason to be worried," said Myrtle.

"Are there any more? I'm still wondering how Elaine is able to manage all these pictures."

"Let's see. One more. Oh my."

Jack held out his hand to Miles and he automatically handed the boy the wilted dandelion with an absent smile. "What is it?"

"It's a picture of Winnie Granger."

Miles frowned. "But she's not part of the cast."

"Let me fill you in on what happened this morning." And she did.

Once she had told Miles all about Winnie's visit that morning, Myrtle added, "And I think she must be at the theater to create a scene of some kind."

Miles said, "She should watch her back. She seems to be messing with completely the wrong people. One of them is a killer."

"She carefully told me that she's getting a really large dog."

"What was the point in going to this meeting? How would she even *know* about the meeting?" asked Miles.

"The same way she knew I was awake very early this morning. She walked by and saw my lights on. She probably walked by the theater and saw all the cars there. Elaine will have to fill us in as to what she was doing there, but if I had to guess, it has something to do with the fact that she feels resentful that she can't mourn Roscoe openly and that their relationship was a secret." Myrtle held out her hand so that Jack could jump down off a backpacking gnome.

"How big is this dog?" asked Miles.

"Rottweiler. She needs to pick it up from the breeder, though."

"Hope it's not a puppy," murmured Miles.

Jack now appeared to be done with being outside. He indicated this by leaving the two of them in the backyard and running to the door and inside the house.

Miles gave Myrtle a look. "I do love Jack. But he appears to have more energy this morning than I do. Actually, he appears to have more energy than an adrenaline fueled battalion going into combat."

"Let's see. What time is it?" Myrtle tried to look at her watch but had had such a discombobulated morning that she hadn't put it on.

"I don't think it's nap time. Do three year olds even *take* naps?" asked Miles. He glanced at his own watch. "It's ten-fifty."

"I don't think they do in the mornings anymore. Let's take Jack on a field trip into town. He can get an ice cream at the diner. It's almost eleven. By the time we walk over there, Bo's Diner will have opened for lunch," said Myrtle.

JACK WAS DELIGHTED to put his shoes on and go out for ice cream. Myrtle decided to change into some dry clothes before they left since she was still damp from all the ice fishing. The trick was to keep up with Jack. Miles gave her an alarmed look as they half-ran toward the diner. "Need to borrow my cane, Miles?" asked Myrtle a bit breathlessly. She held Jack's hand with one hand, her cane with the other.

"I need to borrow an electric scooter. No wonder Elaine is so slender," said Miles, breathing rather heavily.

They were walking up to the diner when Myrtle's phone chirped at her from her purse. She said, "Miles, can you grab my phone? I don't have a free hand."

Miles got the phone and this time managed to work it. "It's Elaine again. She says that the cast meeting is over and she's on the way to pick up Jack."

"Tell her that we're downtown getting Jack an ice cream and will text her when we're all done," said Myrtle. Miles gave her a tired look and she said, "Well, I can't renege on the ice cream, Miles. I don't think we'd like the consequences. You know that! You've got grandchildren, too."

"My grandchildren are teenagers. And they live on the other side of the country," said Miles.

"They weren't *always* teenagers, surely."

"But they did always live on the other side of the country," said Miles a little sadly.

"See? Time spent with Jack is good for you. Let's get him settled with an ice cream and we'll pick up lunch to go. I'm willing to share my grandchild with you."

And despite Miles's protestations to the contrary, he did seem to be enjoying himself with Jack. Miles somehow dug up an old sleight of hand trick from long ago and was entertaining Jack with it as Myrtle ordered a chocolate ice cream, two pimento cheese chili dogs, and a chicken salad and fruit at the counter.

After ordering, she turned to see that Miles was making a "look behind you" expression at her. She turned to see Veronica Parsley there.

Veronica, who had been looking slightly bored, suddenly perked up a little. "Oh. The reporter and her photographer. It was ... Edna?"

"Myrtle," said Myrtle. "And Miles."

"Looks like you've taken on a young apprentice," she said, eyes softening a bit as she looked at Jack.

Jack beamed sunnily at her.

Whatever it took to loosen Veronica up. Myrtle was ready to take advantage of it. "Isn't he a darling boy? He's our little investigative reporting sidekick." She quickly segued before it was Veronica's turn in line.. "I was so *shaken* to hear about the tragedy of Roscoe's death. What can you tell me about it?"

Veronica looked a little cagey. "I don't want to go on the record, you know."

"We can use 'source who wishes to remain unnamed.' That will work fine," said Myrtle.

Miles took out his phone to maintain the fiction of being a photographer and half-heartedly took a couple of pictures of Veronica. Since he was sitting on a bench next to Jack, Myrtle had a feeling that the angle of the photos was going to be rather odd.

"As I told you both yesterday, I *did* return to the theater last night." She paused for effect. "And I'd have been a real idiot to have told the press my intentions for returning to the theater if I'd had an intention at all of killing someone there."

Myrtle preened a bit at being called *the press*. "Certainly." Although Myrtle thought perhaps she hadn't *intended* on killing someone at the theater, at the time she was admitting to planning to return there.

"So I was at the theater and did some work there—fixed a few set pieces that needed repair. And I practiced my lines a bit while I was there. It never hurts to practice on a stage, you know," said Veronica.

Miles glanced at Myrtle. Veronica's tone was a touch defensive.

"Anyway, I finished up and left. I didn't get everything done that I needed to, but I was so exhausted that I figured I'd set my clock really early and take care of it first thing in the morning. I did lock the door behind me. I was pulling out of the parking lot when I spotted Skip Rogers heading toward the theater. I thought that was sort of odd, you know?"

Miles cleared his throat and asked, "Skip doesn't help mend sets?"

"Not a bit. For all of his talk about devotion to the theater, he sure doesn't seem to care about the nuts and bolts of it all. As far as I know, there was absolutely no reason at all for him to be there. To me, that seems a little bit suspicious," said Veronica. When she saw Miles point his phone in her direction, she immediately erased the lines between her brows and gave him a wide grin. Then she hesitated. "Wait a minute. We said this would be off the record."

"It's just a shot for our files," said Myrtle, giving Miles a quelling look. "In case we need a photo in the future."

Jack carefully pulled Miles's phone out of his hand and bent over it, swiping his small fingers across the screen. Miles, absorbed in either Veronica's tale or her beauty, didn't notice what Jack was doing.

Before Myrtle could ask anything else, it was both Veronica's turn to be seated and time for Myrtle to pick up their takeout.

She thrust the takeout bag at Miles and bent to hand Jack the ice cream. She'd thought about putting it in a cup for the walk home, but Jack had asked for a cone and cones *were* more fun to eat. "Are we all set, then? Let's head back to Nana's house."

"P-Yano? P-Yano?" asked Jack intently as they headed out the door of the diner and onto the few wooden stairs. He held the ice cream cone with both hands and turned to look up at Myrtle.

Myrtle quizzically glanced at Miles. Under her breath she asked, "Do you understand him?"

"Me? You're the expert here."

She was about to give him a sharp retort when suddenly a great howl came from Jack. "Mercy!" gasped Myrtle as Jack lay sprawled at the bottom of the short staircase. He'd fallen right on his hands and knees on the gravelly parking lot and his ice cream was all over the ground. Myrtle devoutly hoped that the howling was more due to the condition of the ice cream than Jack's knees.

She used her cane to quickly get all the way down on the ground. "Jack?" she asked, pulling him gently into her lap.

Miles winced. "Two skinned knees. Ugh. Haven't had a skinned knee in fifty-five years, but it's amazing how it all comes back to you."

"Well, now he's definitely not going to want to walk back," clucked Myrtle. "Do get the car, Miles."

"Don't you want me to help you get him cleaned up first?" asked Miles.

"Ice cweam," cried Jack.

"Or go in for another ice cream?" asked Miles, surveying the sad scene of the spilled ice cream.

"But it's going to take you a while to walk back for the car," said Myrtle.

"Can I help?" asked a deep voice from below them.

Myrtle glanced up and saw Blaine Prevost. "Any help would be fantastic," said Myrtle over Jack's crying.

Blaine was already pulling a couple of carefully-folded tissues out of his pocket. "Clean, I promise," he said, stooping down to carefully clear the dirt and gravel out of Jack's skinned knees.

"Did your ice cream fall down?" he gently asked Jack.

Jack, surprised by the sudden appearance, just nodded. The crying was thankfully subsiding into hiccups.

"That's about as much as I can do without water to rinse it out. Let me run inside and grab some wet paper towels and maybe ask for some bandages." Then he gave Jack a big smile. "Do you want another chocolate ice cream? Or another flavor?"

Jack seemed intrigued by the idea of another flavor. Myrtle was pretty sure she hadn't mentioned the possibility of any flavors other than chocolate or vanilla. Sometimes it was best not to confuse the issue when one was dealing with toddlers.

"'nother kind?" asked Jack.

"Maybe mint chocolate chip?" asked Blaine with another grin.

Jack thought for a second and then nodded.

"Excellent choice. Back in a second." And Blaine disappeared into the diner.

Miles was already walking away. "On my way to get the car," he called behind him.

"P-yano!" said Jack loudly.

"And keep mulling over that particular word, please, and its possible definitions!" said Myrtle.

Blaine, unmarried and childless though he was, had somehow been able to completely engage Jack and bring back his usual sunny self. Maybe it was because he'd been so decisive. Decisive, but also willing to hand over some of the decision-making to Jack. After all, wasn't it what most people wanted—to be more in control? It was true for Myrtle and she figured it was probably true for Jack, too. Now Jack was fascinated with his skinned knees, which had fortunately stopped bleeding and now just looked sort of gross.

Blaine was back in only a minute or two with some damp paper towels. And, for some reason, Bo's Diner had superhero bandages. Perhaps they'd been on sale at the store. At any rate, Jack clearly thought that *Blaine* was the superhero now. He carefully cleaned up Jack's knees, patted them down with another dry paper towel, and then cautiously applied the adhesive bandages.

As soon as that was done, one of the waitresses opened the door to the diner. "Poor baby," she said, words full of sympathy but eyes only for the handsome Blaine. "Here's your ice cream, sweetie." It was now, most helpfully, in a cup instead of a cone.

Blaine hopped up and took it from the now-blushing waitress with a gleaming grin. He presented it to Jack with a flourish, making Jack giggle.

With Jack now safely absorbed in his ice cream, Myrtle relaxed a little. She gave Blaine a relieved look as she scooted back from her crouch until she could sit on one of the wooden steps.

"Thank you a million times over. Wow. You saved the day ... and perfect timing, too."

Blaine smiled back at her and then looked a bit reflective. "I'm glad I could do something to help. I've felt sort of ... I guess rather impotent lately, in the face of being helpless to stop the bizarre and tragic rash of violence over at the theater." He shifted uncomfortably and gave a faint and wistful smile at Jack's utter enthusiasm in his enjoyment of the ice cream.

Myrtle nodded. "I was so sorry to hear what had happened at the theater last night. I didn't know Roscoe well, but I thought he seemed like quite the gentleman."

Blaine looked slightly surprised at this, as she hoped he would. She was definitely hoping to get a little more insight from him. "A gentleman?" He colored a little. "I'm sorry, it's just that under the circumstances, that word is surprising. Considering his, ah, infidelity."

"You mean the affair with Nandina?" asked Myrtle innocently.

Blaine shook his head. "I'm afraid it looks like we were all wrong about an affair with Nandina. No, you see, we had a cast meeting this morning and a woman showed up saying that *she* had been having an affair with Roscoe."

"A woman you knew?" asked Myrtle.

"Her name is Winnie Granger. I was acquainted with her for years, although she hasn't done much with the theater for a while. I think that's because her job as a pharmacist keeps her busy. Anyway, she was there this morning, very upset. She insisted that *she* was the aggrieved party in this whole thing and seemed very indignant about Josie being in charge of funeral plans."

Myrtle said, "Why was that?"

"Because she thought Josie had done it," said Blaine, looking at Myrtle levelly. "Don't we all?"

"Josie *did* have a strong motive."

Blaine raised his eyebrows. "The fact that she was insanely jealous over Roscoe? Most definitely. But I think we can't automatically label her the murderer. Someone else wanted Nandina gone. Skip."

Myrtle said, "Because he was in love with Nandina and was despondent that she didn't return his feelings. Why would Skip kill Roscoe, though?"

"Maybe Roscoe was blackmailing Skip. Maybe he knew that Skip killed Nandina and he was using that information against him," said Blaine.

"But Roscoe is married to a wealthy woman." Myrtle absently smiled at Jack as he gave her an ice cream-covered grin.

"That he wanted to divorce. Let's face it, money was probably the *only* thing holding Roscoe back from leaving Josie for Winnie. Maybe he thought he could get enough money out of Skip to finally walk out of his marriage," said Blaine.

Myrtle tilted her head to the side. "Well ... I suppose. It all seems a little too convenient to me."

Blaine said in a low voice, "Do you think I just dreamed this all up? When I left last night from the theater, I'd carefully made sure to clean up the clutter on the stage so we'd be ready for our next practice and performance. When I was at the theater this morning, I saw Skip's wallet there. So at some time last night, Skip came back to the theater."

This was definitely food for thought. But Myrtle didn't have time to munch on it because Miles pulled up. Miles actually pulled up *directly* in front of them as if unsure whether Jack could make it even a few yards with his skinned up knees. And he'd apparently been thinking on the assignment that Myrtle had tasked him with.

"I think I know what he means," said Miles rather excitedly as he got out of the car. "P-Yano. Piano. He wants to play my piano."

"Does he even know you have a piano?" asked Myrtle doubtfully. "It's not as if you play it. There's no music wafting out of your house at all hours of the day and night or anything. The piano, as a matter of fact, seems purely decorative."

Miles said stiffly, "I do know how to play it. And Jack came over and played it not very long ago when you were watching him. Remember?"

Myrtle frowned. "Not very long ago. Hmm. Oh, I do remember. Although that was *last winter*. That's pretty long ago. Okay. We'll have your piano be the grand finale then." She watched as Blaine gave Jack a high five (a sticky one, since Jack was now covered in ice cream), and swung him around in the air and then up into Miles's Volvo until Jack was giggling.

"Blaine, I don't know how to thank you," said Myrtle.

"Me either," said Miles fervently. "Things were going downhill fast."

Blaine said, "It was my pleasure." And then he hurried into the diner.

CHAPTER FOURTEEN

"I'M BORROWING YOUR phone to text Elaine to say we're heading to your house. My phone is buried somewhere in my purse. And I guess I should tell Elaine about Jack's little accident. I hate to return him in worse shape than he was when he was dropped off," fretted Myrtle.

Miles said, "I'm sure she's used to it. Toddlers aren't known for coordination and dexterity."

"Neither are seniors," grunted Myrtle as she tipped over her water reaching for Miles's phone. "Can I not get a break from water today?" After quickly sopping up that spill she finally picked up his phone. And frowned. "What's wrong with this thing?"

"Did it have water spilled on it?" asked Miles glumly.

"Not a drop. It's turning on fine, but there isn't an icon for texting," said Myrtle, peering very hard at the phone screen.

"There must be," said Miles, reaching for the phone.

"Ah! Not while we're in motion. Here, pull into your driveway and I'll show you. It also looks like you don't have an icon to make phone calls," said Myrtle.

"But it's a phone! It *must* make phone calls."

"Not according to what I'm seeing on this screen," said Myrtle.

Miles pulled into the driveway and quickly retrieved his phone. He pushed his glasses up his nose and stared intently at his home screen. Then he opened all of his phone's apps and stared at them. "They're ... gone! What happened?"

Myrtle considered this for a moment. "No offense to my darling grandson, but do I recall seeing him playing with your phone while we were in the diner?"

"But Jack wouldn't have been able to delete my phone and messaging apps," said Miles.

Myrtle shook her head. "Don't sell him short, Miles. I've a feeling he knows more about your phone than you do."

"He can't even read!"

Jack beamed at Miles.

"Reading doesn't really factor into it," said Myrtle.

"P-Yano," reminded Jack.

"Yes, that's right. We're going to go in and play Mr. Miles's piano," said Myrtle sedately. "And I'm going to dig my phone from the depths of my pocketbook and call Elaine."

Miles was still fiddling with his phone. "Well, I'll be doggoned."

Myrtle stopped on her way up Miles's front walk. "It looks like Wanda has been by."

"Oh no! No. Not more squash!" Miles finally walked away from the car, still holding his phone and a bag from the diner.

"Squash and a horoscope, I'm presuming. I'm thinking, at this point, that we really need to *deflect* Wanda. I need to give her something else to think about besides paying you back for all your past kindnesses," mulled Myrtle. "Although you'd have thought her new column would have been enough."

"Tell her that the amount of squash I'm receiving is dissuading me from making *future* kindnesses," muttered Miles, giving the large bag of squash a horrified look. "Is she just dumping fertilizer on her garden? How is such an abomination possible?"

"I believe she left a note on it this time," said Myrtle, peering at the bag.

"Can we decipher it? You know what Wanda's writing is like," said Miles. "I don't know how you're managing with your editing of her stuff."

"Her scrawl is short and sweet this time. It says *gif to theeater*." Myrtle paused. "That's odd, isn't it? It's almost as if she knew we were taking the squash there."

"People will start running away screaming when they see us coming with all the squash we're unloading on them," said Miles darkly as he unlocked the door. "Myrtle, you have to take it away with you this afternoon. I can't bear to look at it. Just leave it on the porch so that you can collect it when you go."

"It's not as if squash has a *smell*, Miles," said Myrtle, amused. "It won't contaminate your home if you bring it inside."

"I wouldn't be so sure," said Miles. He watched Jack launch himself joyfully at his piano and start enthusiastically banging on the keys.

Miles took swipes and jabs at his phone screen. Myrtle said impatiently, "Look, why don't you hand the phone back to Jack and go grab a paper towel?"

Miles stared at her. "Both of those ideas surprise me. I can't imagine why I need a paper towel and why give this device back to the perpetrator who rendered it useless?"

"Because Jack's hands are sticky with ice cream and it's probably getting all over your keys. And, since Jack was the one who messed up your phone, perhaps he's the one who can fix it," said Myrtle.

Miles sighed and handed his phone back to the boy. It was, perhaps, the only thing that could distract him from the upright piano. Miles returned promptly with a damp paper towel and Myrtle handed Miles's phone back to him while she carefully wiped Jack's hands clean.

"Well, I'll be," said Miles, staring at his phone. "The messaging and phone is back!"

"I keep telling people that my grandson is a genius. They simply don't listen to me," said Myrtle with a sniff.

Jack resumed his high volume concert and Myrtle motioned Miles to the kitchen. "While he's playing, we know exactly what he's doing. Let's step away until the music stops."

Miles winced at the piano's pained notes. "The word *music* is debatable."

They pulled their food out and sat down at the table, munching thoughtfully. Myrtle washed down a large bite with her drink and then said, "They're all trying to pin it on Skip now."

Miles raised his eyebrows and took a bite from his fruit. "You mean Veronica is. She was the one talking about seeing him come back to the theater when she was leaving."

"Not only Veronica. While we were waiting for you to come back with the car, Blaine also said that Skip was likely to have done it. Well, he did make a mention of Josie too, but Skip in particular. He said that Skip left his wallet at the theater overnight. Proof that he'd been there," said Myrtle.

"I can see why Skip would want to kill Nandina. Sort of. But Skip killing Roscoe?" Miles shook his head.

"Oh, it would have to be a killing-the-blackmailer kind of thing. Blaine suggested that Roscoe wanted money of his own so that he could leave Josie for Winnie. Perhaps Roscoe and Skip set up a meeting for Skip to pay Roscoe to keep him quiet about what Roscoe had *really* seen on stage. You know." Myrtle finished off a pimento cheese dog.

There was a light tap on Miles's front door and they glanced at each other. "Is it Elaine already?" asked Miles.

"I told her I'd text her when we were ready to have Jack picked up," said Myrtle.

"Aren't we, though? Aren't we ready to have Jack picked up?" asked Miles, heading for his front door. "After all, *Tomorrow's Promise* is about to come on. And we rarely watch it live." Miles peeked through the peephole on the door. "Oh no."

Jack became interested in the high notes on the piano, which was fortunate because Myrtle could actually hear Miles's mutter.

"Oh no?"

Miles hurried away from the door toward Myrtle. "It's Erma. I can't handle Erma today."

"You can handle Erma on *other* days? I certainly can't. You'll have to give me tips," said Myrtle with a shudder.

"She wants to show me those horrid vacation photos of hers. I've been avoiding her for a week," said Miles.

"How do you know they're horrid if you haven't seen them?" asked Myrtle innocently.

Miles rolled his eyes at her.

"Helloooo!" came a nasal voice from behind the front door.

"Let's be very quiet," said Miles in a desperate tone.

Jack then discovered the low notes and banged dramatically on them.

Miles rolled his eyes again.

"Go on, you can't hide now. You may as well get it over with. I can text Elaine and tell her to join us in a few minutes. Erma will leave when Elaine arrives," said Myrtle. She took out her phone and sent a quick message.

"Erma doesn't pick up on subtlety. She'll have to be forcibly removed," said Miles glumly.

"Maybe Pasha will follow Elaine over. Erma is terrified of Pasha."

Miles said with a groan, "Erma will spread rumors that we're seeing each other."

"I think I've reached the *I-don't-care-what-people-say* age," said Myrtle with a shrug.

Jack played more dramatic notes with feeling.

"I know you're there!" trilled Erma from outside. "I hear you playing Rachmaninoff."

Myrtle raised her eyebrows. "Jack, you're a prodigy."

Miles reluctantly walked to the door and opened it. "Erma. How are you?"

Erma swept in, gabbing constantly as she did. Erma lived next door to Myrtle and was the sole reason she carefully peered out of her door before walking outside. Also the reason for her privacy fence in the backyard. Myrtle could never decide whether Erma looked more like a donkey or a rat. Perhaps that's because she desperately fled every conversation she was forced to endure with Erma as quickly as possible.

Erma gave her braying laugh. "The best thing about this vacation is that my intestinal issues didn't interfere. As they usually do, you know." She came to a screeching halt and her jaw dropped, revealing a set of prominent teeth. "Well, looka here! It's Myrtle! I get to show *both* of you my vacation pictures."

"You don't seem to have an album with you," said Miles in a tight voice.

Again with the grating, braying laugh. "Silly! No one uses albums anymore. The pictures are on my phone!" She gave Myrtle a sneering smile. "Here visiting your special friend, are you?"

Myrtle bared her teeth in a smile. "I'm here allowing my genius grandson to play Miles's piano. Apparently, he plays Rachmaninoff."

"Are you fond of squash, Erma?" asked Miles hopefully.

"Like the English game?" asked Erma.

"Like the vegetable."

Erma made a face. Or, rather, her face became worse than it already was.

"I guess we'll take it to the theater again," said Miles with a sigh.

Erma was already making herself comfortable in the kitchen. She pulled up the pictures on her phone and thrust the device at Myrtle. "Here. Scroll that way. You can see some great pictures, just wonderful, wonderful pictures. Oh!" Her eyes grew big and she put a hand to her heart. "You could put them in the paper!"

Myrtle's head started to pound. Jack's determined classical wasn't helping, either. She was already pushing Sloan to do her investigative report and she had no intention of torturing him further with Erma's vacation pictures. "The problem, Erma, is that there has to be a balance of some kind between stories with a particular level of news value and fluff pieces."

"Ooh, I kind of like being thought of as fluff!" Erma gave a gaping grin at Myrtle. There was certainly nothing fluffy about Erma.

"Can't you hold onto them at the newsroom and stick them in on a slow news day?" asked Erma.

"I could. Although I'm not sure when that would be, since a killer is working his way through the cast of the *Malaise* production," said Myrtle archly.

Jack hit a crescendo with his playing and Miles winced.

"Say, are you done eating? I'm starved. Can I have some of your fries?" asked Erma, licking her lips and looking at Myrtle's hapless fries.

Myrtle, who had lost her appetite by this time, pushed the fries toward Erma.

With her mouth now full of fries, Erma said, "Put 'em online."

"Excuse me?" asked Myrtle summoning a politeness she didn't feel.

"The pictures. Up online. The *Bugle's* page," said Erma.

Myrtle dutifully looked through the pictures. They appeared to be a collection of Erma selfies in front of a large lake. Likely a somewhat local lake since Myrtle didn't recall being devoid of Erma's unwelcome company for any amount of time recently. She assumed it wasn't the same lake that their yards backed up to. The pictures didn't appear to be newsworthy on any number of fronts, but Myrtle knew Erma to be like a dog with a toy. Or a terrier, perhaps. Once she got hold of something, she didn't let go. "I'll see what I can do, Erma," said Myrtle.

"Miles," called Erma with another large amount of fries in her mouth. "You have to see the pictures."

"Me!" said Jack, abandoning the piano to Myrtle's great relief. She really did need an ibuprofen by this time.

Erma gave him a huge grin and pushed her phone his way. "Want to see the pretty pictures?" Jack took her phone in both hands and disappeared back into the living room.

Erma changed direction a bit. "So, what about this latest caper?"

Miles, apparently rather affronted at Erma's glib description said, "You mean the murders of two innocent people?"

"Yeah, that's right. The theater people. You both investigating as per usual?" Erma's eyes glinted with interest.

"We're looking into it, yes," said Miles. He quickly retrieved napkins and thrust them at Erma as she set about noisily licking her fingers. "Myrtle handles the investigative journalism, of course. I seem to have been taking a lot of pictures."

"You wouldn't have any information on the murders, I suppose," said Myrtle. It pained her to stroke Erma's ego, but occasionally Erma *did* know something. Somehow. It probably had a lot to do with the fact that she was an insufferable gossip.

"As a matter of fact, I might!" Erma beamed at them.

"I thought you were away. Or were away for at least some of the time," said Miles.

"I was. But I'm friends, you know, with the owner of the theater—Mr. Toucan." Erma blushed a bit.

Miles gave Myrtle an incredulous look. Surely Erma and Mr. Toucan weren't a *thing*. Could anyone possibly *have* a *thing* with Erma?

"He's had a very tough time with that theater, let me tell you. He tried to renovate it and the more they did, the more the contractor *found* to do. It all was really, really costly."

"Yes, yes, we know all about that," said Myrtle impatiently.

"Any-hoo, he gets free help wherever he can find it. Your Elaine helps with the box office and other volunteering. I suppose she eventually wants to act?" asked Erma doubtfully.

Myrtle had her own doubts about Elaine's possible acting career, but she certainly wasn't going to admit that to Erma. "Perhaps," she said shortly.

"And the cast helps with the sets—that girl. Veronica?" said Erma.

Veronica would likely be pleased to be called a girl. "Yes."

"So volunteering is going on."

"Yes." Myrtle was getting tired of this.

"And since Mr. Toucan and I are ... well, friends," again with the insufferable blush, "I offered to help him with promo." Erma grinned proudly.

"*You're* helping him with marketing. You've got experience in marketing? I thought you were ... well, I wasn't sure what kind of work you did," said Myrtle.

"I'm a consultant," said Erma. "I can do almost anything on social media or setting up websites, or whatever. And, with that kind of consulting, I can do it from wherever I am. It's how I can spend so much time at home. Which is a blessing. Being at home."

Miles giggled at the idea of Erma's being at home being any kind of blessing. Myrtle shot him a repressive look and he descended into a fit of coughing.

"Okay, so let me get this straight, Erma. You do publicity for Mr. Toucan's theater on different social media. I'm assuming you were also in charge of putting the word out about *Malaise*," said Myrtle.

Erma nodded emphatically. "That's right. And you can look on Twitter and Facebook and see that I put a picture of the cast up and snippets of reviews and that kind of thing. But then something weird happened the night of the murder. Opening night. I was out of town, at the lake. And *somebody* logged into the theater's account and posted something hateful about being a murder there. And there *was* a murder there! Awful."

"Who do you think might have been able to hack into the account and do something like that?" asked Myrtle intently.

"Oh, Veronica. Clearly." Erma polished off the fries.

"Really? Why do you think so?" asked Myrtle.

"Well, *anyone* could have done it. Anyone. Because Toucan has all of his passwords on a sticky note on his monitor. Anyone *could* have done it. But I caught Veronica sneaking around Toucan's office, myself, shortly before I left for my vacation. And she looked very, very guilty," said Erma. "Saying something about Nandina is just the sort of spiteful thing I'd expect Veronica to do."

"So you don't have any *specific* evidence. This is more of a gut feeling," said Miles.

"I've got a good gut," said Erma, patting the protruding item. "And she did have a pencil and paper in her hand. She put down the pencil real quick and scurried away. Fast."

But that, reflected Myrtle, may have had more to do with Erma being Erma. Myrtle scurried away herself as soon as she spotted the woman.

Miles said reasonably, "Just because Veronica put a rather hateful message up on social media about Nandina doesn't mean that she killed her."

Erma blinked at him. "Of course it does."

Myrtle briefly closed her eyes. Miles should know that you never argue with Erma. Never. You just walk away.

"No, no really it doesn't. It's petty, it's mean, but it's nonviolent and non-confrontational. Murdering someone, on the other hand, is not only highly antisocial, it's violent and confrontational. It seems to me as if two different people were responsible," said Miles, his voice rising just a hair.

"No, Miles. Did you see what Veronica put on Twitter? She said Nandina was going to be dead," said Erma stridently.

"Actually, the tweet said nothing of the kind. It said *tonight's production features the better off dead Nandina Marshall*," corrected Myrtle. She was getting weary of this. "Nowhere did it say that Veronica nor anyone else was going to kill Nandina."

Now *Myrtle* was arguing with Erma. Pointless. And Jack decided to start being a virtuoso again.

The upside of Jack playing again was that it appeared to chase off Erma. "I'd better go," she said loudly, over the banging of the keys.

Miles gave Myrtle a relieved look.

"Do you know where my phone is?" asked Erma, looking around her.

"Check in the living room," shouted Myrtle.

"Where?"

"The LIVING ROOM!" repeated Myrtle.

Sure enough, Erma's phone with all her vacation pictures was on Miles's coffee table. Erma reached down to pick it up and, Myrtle supposed, to look fondly at her vacation selfies again. Erma frowned. She hit a few buttons on the device. She frowned again and glanced desperately over at Miles and Myrtle.

"They're gone! My pictures are gone!" she gasped.

Miles said, "They can't be gone. We just saw them."

Myrtle reflected again how little Miles knew about phones ... and toddlers. And the thought of not having to put Erma's vacation pictures up on the *Bugle's* various social media outlets made a smile curl at the edges of Myrtle's mouth. As she had said *many* times before, Jack Clover was an absolute baby genius.

CHAPTER FIFTEEN

ERMA STOMPED OUT WITH her phone not much longer after that.

"Brilliant boy," breathed Myrtle to Jack, who was banging away on the piano keys again.

"Hear, hear," said Miles, holding up his lemonade in a toast.

There was a light tap on Miles's front door and Elaine opened the door. "Knock, knock," she said. She looked behind her before closing the door. "Erma looked sort of peeved. I hope Jack didn't do anything to upset her." Jack ran over from the piano, hugged his mother's legs, and then ran back to the piano to continue what appeared to be an opus.

"Jack thoughtfully erased Erma's vacation pictures so that I didn't have to upload them to the *Bugle*'s social media," said Myrtle.

"Oh. Oh dear. No wonder Erma was a little cool to me on my way in," said Elaine with a sigh.

"Just keep your fingers crossed that continues," said Myrtle.

"How did the cast meeting go?" asked Miles.

"There was a lot of crying," said Elaine. "But then, these were actors."

Myrtle said, "So you think some of the emotion was faked?"

"I'm not sure if they could even help themselves. They act so much, it's like the skill transfers to their regular lives. Veronica's tears were definitely faked. Her eyes were blank. Skip seemed the most genuinely upset to me."

"Skip did?" asked Myrtle. "Because everyone seems to think Skip did it."

Elaine frowned. "I guess he could have. But if he did, he certainly seems sorry about it now. Blaine didn't cry, but maintained this sort of *I'm-going-to-be-strong-for-the-cast* posture."

"How tedious of him," said Myrtle. "The more I get to know these people, the less I like them."

"Cady Flosser was there and seemed distraught and fearful. Like she thought she might be next. Jumpy," said Elaine.

Myrtle said, "We'll have to run by and see her. She wasn't working at the diner, of course, since she was at the meeting."

Miles sighed. "More diner food. I'll need to make an appointment for a checkup after this investigation is through."

"And tell us about Winnie Granger's sudden arrival at the meeting," prompted Myrtle.

"It was very dramatic. But then, she has a background in the theater, too," said Elaine. "She swept in, tears in her eyes. She called out anyone who appeared to be grieving, saying that no one had the right to grieve more than she did. Winnie seemed furious, as if she had been shortchanged somehow."

Myrtle said, "Well, she *was*. But not by the cast members. By Roscoe. He was the one who was determined to keep their relationship a secret. And the fact that he *did* keep it a secret might have resulted in Nandina's death. If jealous Josie is the murderer, that is."

"I'm not sure if she's the murderer or not, but she's certainly efficient. Roscoe's funeral is tomorrow," said Elaine.

"Tomorrow!" chorused Miles and Myrtle.

Myrtle added, "The state police didn't need to do any forensic work?"

Elaine shook her head. "Not according to Red. It was pretty cut and dried. Roscoe was struck with a blunt instrument and then was pushed down the stairs. There was no forensic work needed for that. As far as any physical evidence at the site, I think there was tons since everyone used that exit and entrance. Anyway, the funeral is tomorrow morning at Grace Hill. Graveside service at eleven o'clock."

"Whatever happened to Nandina's service?" asked Myrtle with a frown. "Did I skip that one somehow? Surely the state is done with her body."

"Her family came into town very briefly to claim her body. She was cremated and there was no memorial service," said Elaine.

"How awful," muttered Myrtle. "That's not the Southern way. Cremate all you like, but have a memorial service, for heaven's sake."

"Followed by a small reception by the family," added Miles.

"Exactly. With ham salad sandwiches with the crusts cut off and pasta salad. What's wrong with people these days?" asked Myrtle.

Perhaps sensing that a change of subject was required, Elaine said, "Going back to the cast meeting, I did also notice that Mr. Toucan was very distraught about the events. He was practically wringing his hands. He was sad about Nandina and Roscoe from a personal point of view, I think, but he was also thinking about the fact that he'd lost two of his most popular, versatile actors."

"Was Nandina versatile?" asked Miles doubtfully. "I'd have thought she was already typecast."

"She did have a little range. But we had to do a lot of make-up and costume work to get her to look frumpy or something," said Elaine.

"I can imagine," said Myrtle.

"And I think Mr. Toucan was also upset that people might be worried about *going* to the theater now, with all the negative publicity. Basically, he was concerned about the bottom line," said Elaine.

"I'm concerned that he's possibly dating Erma Sherman," said Myrtle, making a face. "Or so Erma is leading me to believe. At any rate, I can't believe he's involved in any way in these murders. He just doesn't have a motive. He'd have a motive to kill the *murderer* to stop all the disruptions at his theater, but he had no cause to murder Nandina or Roscoe."

Jack came up to Elaine and laid his head against her leg. "I think somebody is ready for nap time," she said.

"I think *I'm* ready for nap time," said Miles.

Jack and Elaine left and Miles plopped down in a brown leather armchair. "This morning has been exhausting. I don't know how Elaine does it."

"Youth is on her side," said Myrtle with a shrug. "So, should we pick up our investigating tomorrow at the funeral?"

"That's not exactly good funeral etiquette."

"We'll be discreet. And we might be able to pick up some good clues. It's always interesting to watch people's expressions at funerals. Particularly when one of them is a killer," said Myrtle.

"Red will probably be there," said Miles cautiously. "Won't he be able to tell that you're poking around in the case?"

"I'll just tell him I'm catching up with people," said Myrtle with a sniff. "He should be too busy to worry about what I'm doing. Now, I think I'm ready to completely relax. Until I have to turn in my story on Roscoe's murder and Winnie's involvement with him. And Wanda's new horoscope," she added with a sigh.

"So I'll see you tomorrow morning," said Miles.

"No, no. It's time to watch *Tomorrow's Promise*. We can turn our brains completely off."

And they did.

Myrtle found the task of writing the story about Roscoe's death most taxing on her. Usually it took her only minutes to compose a well-worded factual account of an event, but today it took her quite a bit longer. She had the feeling it had something to do with the fact that she had to include the bit about Winnie in there and leave it up to the readers to make inferences. Myrtle made the article as factual and as undramatic as she possibly could. She made a face and put *staff* at the top instead of her own byline. She'd prefer not to own up to this one.

Then she set to work on Wanda's column that she'd left with the squash. She'd gone all out on this one, she could tell. She'd even tried for a bit of imagery with her "*the starz in the nite sky done tole me bout*" something. Myrtle sighed. How many of Wanda's words to leave in and how many to take out? At least it made for entertaining reading. This was not writing that would put anyone to sleep. One of Wanda's edited forecasts proclaimed that John Lazenbee needed to keep his shoelaces tied better.

The ringing of the phone startled Myrtle and she jumped. "Hello?" she asked a bit crankily. It was never fun to be surprised.

"Miss Myrtle?" came a jocular voice on the other end. "It's Sloan. Listen, I've had some terrific feedback from Wanda the Wonderful's first horoscope. She's right on the money, isn't she? Fred Culpepper told me that she said he needed to count his change. He counted his change after he'd grocery shopped and sure enough, he was short!"

"That's great, Sloan." Perhaps she should keep those personal references in there, even though they didn't apply to anyone else.

"What's more, I did go ahead and call the plumber. Felt so silly, you know, since I couldn't even tell him what was wrong. I couldn't even tell him what *property* it was on, since it could have been an issue at my house or at the office. But the plumber found it right away. Water was coming right out of a pipe in my ceiling at home. I didn't know, since I never go into that room. She probably saved me from the ceiling caving in!" Sloan's voice was almost agitated in its excitement. "Have you got more?"

"As it happens, I have both Wanda's column and a story of my own on the Roscoe Ragsdale murder. I'm about to email them to you," said Myrtle. It would be easy enough to finish up editing Wanda's piece. Now she knew to keep most of it in there.

"You've got a story?" asked Sloan, a worried tone to his voice.

"Now don't worry. It's a very interesting article and it includes a quotation from someone who claims to have had a clandestine relationship with Roscoe."

"Is that so?" Sloan sounded reluctantly intrigued. "It's just that Red isn't going to be happy about it."

"I used *staff* as my byline," said Myrtle.

"Did you?" The relief in Sloan's voice was palpable. "Well, then! All right, I'll look forward to both of them."

"And I'll have something else for you soon. I'm attending Roscoe's funeral tomorrow and I'm hoping that things in this investigation are starting to come together," said Myrtle. "I know it'll make for a great story."

There was a sigh on the other end. "Yes. All right, Miss Myrtle. Thanks."

The weather the next morning was dreary. Usually funerals in the South were not at all like Hollywood movies. They were usually sunny occasions. The weather would be sunny, sometimes insufferably so, and the funeral goers were frequently somewhat sunny, themselves. They'd be telling funny stories about the loved one, smiling through tears. And looking forward to the huge spread of food following the service, since all of the church ladies would bring out their best funeral foods.

The tables would groan with it. This funeral, however, did not look promising.

What was more, Myrtle's funeral dress was apparently unprepared for the occasion. She had decided that the dress was completely obstinate. Myrtle *knew* that when she was finished, each time, with her funeral dress that she carefully cleaned it and put it back into her closet to be prepared for the next tragic event. However, whenever it was removed from that closet, it would either be missing a button, have a hem falling out, or sport evidence of some sort of gravy stain. As if she ever ate gravy at a funeral reception! She knew better. Myrtle was convinced the dress sabotaged itself in protest.

This time the dress had deliberately made itself too snug. Myrtle knew herself to be a lady with big bones but the dress had *always* fit before. This time it was quite obviously too tight around her waist and hips. Snarling at the offending item, she took it off and stuffed it back in the closet. With the rain, perhaps black slacks would be better anyway. She stared into her closet for inspiration and finally decided on a black striped blouse to go with the slacks. The scratchiness of the blouse was somewhat annoying too, but there weren't many funeralesque choices.

She was still trying to locate her errant lipstick when Miles tapped at her front door. She stomped over to open it and Miles walked in, shaking his wet umbrella off on her front porch before he did. She left to find the makeup and he called after her, "Where's the funeral dress? Is it misbehaving again?"

"It shrank itself," she hollered back. "And now my lipstick has gone AWOL. This morning isn't looking promising."

"And now we're following up a bad morning with a funeral," said Miles. "It's definitely not hopeful that things will start looking up."

"Found it," she said, a bit breathlessly, hurrying from the back of the house. "Somehow it ended up under my bedside table. I swear I have urchins in my house that hide things."

"I don't know about that, but you did have a Jack in your house that could have filled that bill yesterday. Who knows what he might have been doing when your back was turned," said Miles.

"My back is never turned when I'm watching Jack," said Myrtle a little huffily. "Oh, wait. I was going to bring something to the reception after the funeral. And we still haven't made it to the grocery store! I ate ancient turkey last night with relish on the side. It was an odd meal. You'll need to take me, since I don't want Red to know that I need to shop again."

"So, my question is, what on earth are you going to take to the reception? If there *is* one. Josie, somehow, doesn't seem like the entertaining sort to me," said Miles.

Myrtle was in the kitchen, rooting through her pantry. "She *has* to. For the sake of the mourners. That's the Southern way. The bereaved must host the hoards following the funeral. I don't really know what I'm bringing, no. Nothing from the fridge, I know that. It'll have to be something from the pantry. Let's see. I have olives. What do you think? Olives?"

"Are they serving martinis at the reception? Because otherwise I can't really see olives fitting in there," said Miles. "Unless they're the fancy kind. The kind stuffed with blue cheese or some such."

"Hmm. No, these aren't stuffed. Well, they *are*, technically. With pimentos," said Myrtle, sounding hopeful.

"I just don't think that's going to work," said Miles. "You'd at least have to put them on one of those skinny olive plates or something. To show it was all planned."

"Olive plate? Miles, you amaze me with your party acumen. Actually, why don't *you* be the one to bring something to the reception? Otherwise, it's going to be either olives or cream corn on my part," said Myrtle.

Miles said, "That means we'll have to go back to my place. I'm not really sure what I can whip up in time. We need to get going to this funeral, Myrtle."

"It will only take a minute! We'll run in and grab something," said Myrtle.

Ten minutes later, they were climbing back into Miles's Volvo with granola bars.

"Clearly you need to go to the store too, Miles. I've never seen your kitchen in such a bachelor state before. Usually you have all kinds of goodies in there," said Myrtle. "That's the top item on our to-do list just as soon as we finish our funeral-going. Honestly, I think my olives would have been better, under the circumstances. We're not going to a marathon; we're going to a funeral reception."

"Sounds like a fun day," said Miles gloomily as he brushed off raindrops from his suit sleeve and pulled out of his driveway.

It took them fifteen minutes to arrive at Grace Hill cemetery. Miles, as usual, drove rather sedately. They entered the cemetery gates and passed kudzu-engulfed trees that looked like leafy ghosts reaching out toward the moss-covered graves. The wind blew rain at the windshield. "We've entered a horror movie set," grumbled Miles. "The gloom and graves are setting the scene today."

"Just hurry," said Myrtle. "They're probably already getting started with the service."

"Do we even know where we're going?" asked Miles. "This cemetery is a maze."

"We just keep driving until we see a funeral home tent."

Miles drove for a minute and said, "There's one."

Myrtle peered at the people. "Couldn't be the right service. Those people aren't the right people."

"How on earth can you even tell from such a distance?" asked Miles.

"Because I can see the white hair blowing around from here. That's an old person's funeral. Keep driving around. The road winds around through here forever. This cemetery has been around for one hundred and fifty years. There are acres and acres to go," said Myrtle.

Miles's fingers tightened on the wheel.

A few minutes later they found another funeral home tent and more miserable looking people in dark clothing gathered near it. "That's the one," said Myrtle, leaning forward in her seat. "That's it. I can see Josie looking sour."

"There's no room under the tent," said Miles with a sigh. "I'd hoped Roscoe hadn't enough family to fill the tent."

"If I look frail and pitiful enough, someone will offer me a seat under there," said Myrtle.

"I suppose I could try that," said Miles.

"You haven't enough wrinkles. It only works if you have wrinkles," said Myrtle.

"But *you* don't really have wrinkles," said Miles.

"Yes, but I'm an extremely old woman. That trumps everything. If you're *not* very old, nor a woman, you must produce wrinkles."

Miles pulled out his umbrella from the back of the car. "I'd better prepare for the rain then."

As Myrtle had predicted, a middle-aged man immediately spotted her standing in the rain and gallantly offered her his seat. Miles huddled under his umbrella and hoped the minister wouldn't end up being wordy.

Myrtle glanced around her. Veronica and Skip had somehow gotten seats under the tent. Blaine and Cady were standing outside the tent near Miles. There were some of librarians there that Myrtle recognized, obviously supporting Josie. Fortunately, the minister did seem the succinct type. Or else Josie hadn't wanted a very long service, either way.

Red stood stiffly on the fringes of the gathering. He gave her a curt nod and then continued studying the proceedings.

As it was, the seat offered Myrtle a wonderful view of the service and of Roscoe's grieving widow. Although, Josie looked more angry than grief-stricken.

They were just getting to *ashes to ashes and dust to dust* when the sound of a very loud car engine disrupted the respectful silence. Josie twisted around to stare disapprovingly at the vehicle and then blanched. Her pale face was quickly replaced by a blotchy red one as Winnie Granger stepped out of the small, old, red car.

"What's *she* doing here?" hissed Josie through her teeth. "And she's wearing the same *dress* as me!" As if that were the worse offense.

The people seated around her appeared completely oblivious as to the reason Josie wouldn't want to see Winnie at Roscoe's funeral. As the minister continued talking, Josie rose and strode over to Winnie. Miles unobtrusively stepped backward to better witness the potential altercation.

But there was no need, because the altercation moved to center stage. The women faced off in the rain in the same exact black dress. "How *dare* you come to this funeral!" bellowed Josie.

Winnie said sharply in return, "How dare you play the part of the grieving widow! You're the one who put Roscoe in that coffin. *You* should have been in the theater, not Roscoe."

"You lie!" Josie's face twisted with fury.

Red moved from the perimeter of the funeral and next to the two women. Myrtle saw his cautious face. He clearly wanted them to continue their dialogue, but was prepared to stop them if things got out of hand.

Myrtle felt somewhat sorry for the minister, who couldn't seem to choose between continuing the service or stopping it. He gripped the sides of his pulpit as if divining strength from it and started and stopped his eulogy like a car trying to turn its engine over.

Winnie said, "You did this! You knew Roscoe was being unfaithful, but you looked in the wrong direction. At Nandina!"

Josie snorted. "Well, of *course* I thought it was Nandina. I'd never have guessed it was *you*. And even after reading the story in the paper today, I find it hard to believe." She gave Winnie's very ordinary looks a sneer.

Clearly, the story Myrtle had emailed Sloan had run this morning.

"Why not? If you think about it, you and I look remarkably alike!" said Winnie furiously to the librarian.

Red was shifting from foot to foot, waiting to hear if any revelations occurred, but also ready to pounce if needed. Glancing around at the gathered people, everyone looked completely shocked at this argument in the middle of the funeral service. The most shocked was Miles. He was giving longing glances at his Volvo as if he were dying to escape. Myrtle frowned at him.

"Everyone kept acting as if I was this really paranoid person. 'Roscoe loves you, Josie! He's not seeing anyone! You're being silly.' That's what everyone said. But I'd see Roscoe sneaking text messages on the sly and looking guilty. I knew what was going on. I was only mistaken about who the woman was. And I did *not* kill Nandina!" Josie flushed. "Maybe *you* did! Maybe *you* were jealous of her for working so close with Roscoe."

CHAPTER SIXTEEN

MYRTLE SAW RED LIFT an eyebrow over this and glance back over at Winnie.

An old woman sitting next to Myrtle said, "How common this is. And revolting. Aren't you so completely—"

"Shh!" said Myrtle and leaned closer in to hear the argument.

Winnie laughed at Josie's accusation. "First of all, that doesn't make any sense. Roscoe found Nandina to be a very shallow person. He was *not* attracted to her. In fact, he was furious at her for ... well, something she was doing. What's more, I would *never* have killed Roscoe. I loved him!" Her voice broke a little and she continued quickly, in a harsher tone. "Second of all, I do have an alibi for both murders. I was working a night shift at the pharmacy for both of the nights in question. They've been low on staff. Check it out. Do *you* have proof where *you* were during the murders?"

Josie bit her lip, eyes sulky.

Both women were dripping wet from the rain at this point.

"I thought not!" said Winnie, eyes blazing. "Which is why this service is such a travesty! It should be a celebration of Roscoe's life. A tender service! Why don't you take your seat and I'll take over from here. I'm giving his eulogy."

Josie looked as if she'd received a physical slap in the face. And at this point, Red did step in. "I'm afraid," he said in a quiet and polite voice, "that's not going to happen. You'll quietly stand here at the back and not cause trouble. You see, you didn't pay for this service. And you won't be allowed to disturb it any further."

Winnie opened her mouth as if to argue more, but when she saw the stubbornness on Red's face, she stopped, lowered her head, and gave a quick nod.

Miles appeared vastly relieved. He removed a pocket handkerchief and mopped his forehead with it.

The rest of the service was uneventful. Josie resumed her seat. The minister resumed his rather dry but mercifully short eulogy. There were no further outbursts. Winnie was quiet, but tearful, toward the back of the group.

Myrtle was starting to fret over the rain. If the rain continued at its current level (Cats and Dogs, with possible upgrade to Epic Flooding in the works), no one would stand around and chat. And Myrtle wasn't at all sure who was planning on going to Josie's house for a reception afterward. As a matter of fact, taking a look at Josie's still-furious face, Myrtle wondered if Josie were even entertaining the thought of entertaining.

This explains why, at the end of the service, Myrtle was one of the first people to speak with Josie. "The service was ... touching," said Myrtle, struggling to actually encapsulate the service into words. "But I wondered what your plans were now."

Josie, who'd had a tight smile on her face when Myrtle started speaking to her, gave a baffled frown. "Plans? Now? I suppose to head off to bed with a Bloody Mary or something. What a nerve-wracking day."

"What about a reception?" asked Myrtle.

"Reception?" Josie looked blankly at Myrtle.

"Yes. Usually the family hosts a small reception after the service. For the close friends and family."

Josie's mouth twisted. "Roscoe didn't have much family and nor do I. As for friends?" Her eyes cynically scanned the assembled group. "Are these friends or just curiosity-seekers? Wait, now, explain this again. You're saying that in *this town*, the bereaved are forced to entertain a bunch of gawkers? At their home?"

"Yes. Although we don't usually look at it that way. It's supposed to be a pleasant gathering to remember the deceased. So that people can pay their respects, you see. With lots of really heavy food," said Myrtle. "But you don't *supply* the food. The church ladies descend upon your house with it. And they take over your kitchen. They're very bossy, but incredibly efficient and effective. You don't have to do a thing." Myrtle really wanted to ensure that she would have an opportunity to at least speak to one cast member that day. It seemed as though the reception would be the best bet.

"Oh. I guess that's why I got that phone call from that woman from the church. She said something about fried chicken and green bean casserole," said Josie in the thoughtful voice of one trying to recall a phone conversation that one wasn't really paying attention to at the time. Then she clutched her head so abruptly that Myrtle jumped. "I just can't bear it. What if *that woman* comes over? I don't want to make small talk. I just want to lie down. And the house isn't really ready for visitors."

"How about if I play hostess for you and explain. I can get one of the church ladies to help me, too. That way everyone can come by, bring food, whatever, and you can rest," said Myrtle.

A more pleasant expression crossed Josie's features.

"That will work. Yes, that would be perfect. Thank you," said Josie. "They'll really go there after this?" Myrtle nodded. "Okay. Here, let me give you my key so that you can get a head start." Then she turned to face the mourners.

Myrtle squeezed her way out of the row and out from the tent. The rain was still pouring and she hurried to huddle under Miles's completely inadequate umbrella coverage. "Let's go."

Miles blinked rapidly before automatically following his instructions. "Won't we stick around and talk to the suspects?"

"In this rain? No one will be here. No, we're going to host the reception at Josie's house. She's not from around here and hasn't apparently gone to any funerals while she's *been* here," said Myrtle.

"How is that even possible?" mused Miles. "People kick the bucket left and right in this town."

"Maybe she just didn't opt to go to the funerals of the people she knew. Pity. Everyone knows you've got to pay it forward. Go to other people's funerals so that people will come to yours," said Myrtle as she picked up the pace to Miles's car.

"Does that even make sense?" asked Miles.

"You know what I mean. It's just good karma," said Myrtle. She added, "What do you think about the whole Winnie thing?"

"It was tacky. I don't care what you think, you can't just go in and mess up a funeral service. She obviously is convinced that Josie is responsible," said Miles, sounding prudish.

"It did make the service livelier. And maybe Josie *is* responsible. I'm not sure when we're going to get to interview her. She sounded determined to hole up somewhere in her house during the reception. She gave me a key and told me to play hostess. Let's see if we can get there in a flash and let the ladies from the church in."

But the ladies had already arrived when they pulled up. The first one Myrtle saw was Claudia Prentemps, distinctive by her helmet of gray hair, sprayed into rigid compliance with Aqua Net.

"Sometimes it just doesn't pay to get out of the bed," muttered Myrtle.

"What's wrong now?" asked Miles.

"That's Claudia Prentemps. She's the bossiest church lady of all. She rules with an iron fist," said Myrtle with a groan. "At least the rain seems to have temporarily stopped. She probably ordered it stopped."

"You make her sound like a communist dictator," said Miles with a small smile.

"She *is* a communist dictator! She, in fact, is more qualified to be one than anybody. She'll commandeer the entire kitchen. She'll make snide remarks about our attire. She'll order everyone about. And she'll likely make it very difficult for me to interview murder suspects on her watch. I've had dealings with Claudia before and she is most, *most* challenging to work with," said Myrtle.

"And you're sure she's associated with a *Christian* organization?" asked Miles doubtfully.

"The other church ladies are absolute dolls in comparison. Loving, open, sympathetic, and efficient workers. It's just this *one* person," said Myrtle. "Well, there's no getting around it. Let's get this nightmare over with."

MYRTLE STEPPED OUT of Miles's car, straightening her black and white blouse and wincing at the scratchiness of the material. She stared at her pants, suddenly realizing there appeared to be cat hair on them. How on earth did black cat fur even show *up* on black pants? She wasn't sure, but it was certainly there. The curse of the funeral garments continued. She gritted her teeth into a smile and said, "Claudia. How are you?"

"Ready to help out this poor, bereaved lamb," bellowed Claudia. "Myrtle, good to see you. Have you got the keys to this castle?"

It was indeed a very large house. Myrtle remembered it belonging to an ostentatious mill owner when she was a mere wisp of a girl. She had been to various functions at this home when it belonged to previous owners. As she recalled, each event was extremely hot. She hoped that Josie had updated the air conditioning system when she moved in.

"I have the keys," said Myrtle, holding them up. "Let's get inside before this blasted rain starts up again. Oh. Uh, Claudia, you know Miles—don't you?"

"Indeed not. I don't believe I've had the pleasure," she barked, holding out a hand to Miles. Miles accepted it rather reluctantly as Myrtle fiddled with the lock.

Claudia looked at her askance. "Are you forgetting the food *you* brought?" she asked pointedly.

Miles flushed a little, looking sideways at Myrtle.

"Um, yes. That's right. Miles and I brought granola bars," said Myrtle, a defiant tone in her voice.

Claudia's eyes narrowed and her lips pursed.

Myrtle finally opened the door.

"There! I'll prop the door open and help you unload. Miles will get our granola bars out. Food is in the car?" asked Myrtle.

It was. And it was a tremendous spread. Myrtle couldn't imagine that Josie had been active enough in the local church to qualify for such a feast. Miles and Myrtle made several trips, as did the other ladies who soon drove up. Deviled eggs, ham salad, fried chicken, mac and cheese in a slow cooker. Aspic. Boiled custard and lady fingers.

"This is starting to look more like a wedding than a funeral," muttered Miles, making another trip.

"Except that, in the case of a wedding, someone would likely have cleaned the house. The housework hasn't been done in ages here. Since long before Roscoe's death," said Myrtle.

"Maybe that's because Josie was spending all her time spying on Roscoe," suggested Miles.

"I may have to send Puddin over here," said Myrtle. "Although this is the kind of epic mess that Puddin would turn her nose up at and say that her back was thrown."

Claudia was grimly determined to work her way through the epic mess, preferably before anyone else came over. She grunted as she opened the fridge to put some of the extra casseroles away. "This fridge!" Claudia pulled the kitchen trashcan over to the fridge. "Miles? Take out this trash, would you please? Jane?" she called a hapless and flustered middle-aged woman. "Find the trash bags and pull out a fresh one, would you? Myrtle?"

Claudia looked appraisingly at Myrtle and Myrtle did her best to look fragile. Apparently she did a poor job because Claudia said, "Unload the dishwasher and load it. Wash any excess dishes by hand. I'll sit on the floor here and toss expired items and foods that appear to be old."

Judging from the grunts and groans from Claudia, there was much that appeared to be old. She opened containers, wordlessly exclaimed, and dumped them over into the trashcan. Five minutes later she said, "Miles! Trash again, please! We haven't a moment to spare!"

Claudia turned herself into a mess-fighting machine. She stacked and cleared clutter from the counters. She tossed obvious trash. She scrubbed down counters and the kitchen table. She wiped the fridge. And when more ladies with casseroles appeared, she made sure they were labeled and stored in the freezer or that they were warmed and put on the counter.

"If there were any clues here at all, they've been thrown away," said Miles under his breath to Myrtle.

"I told you what she was like. And she's going to be especially hard on me because I edited an announcement she wrote. Something for the church consignment sale and she was very bitter about the errors I found. This is a woman who doesn't like to be wrong," said Myrtle.

"It looks like I'm on trash duty for the duration," said Miles glumly.

"Certainly not! You'll interview suspects while I'm on kitchen duty."

"What exactly are you going to be doing?" asked Miles.

"Set up, serve, clean up. And likely greet people and thank them on Josie's behalf," said Myrtle, making a face.

"What was that?" asked the commanding voice of Claudia.

"Josie. She won't be attending the reception," said Myrtle loudly in return.

Claudia's features reflected her internal struggle. She was appalled at a hostess ditching the reception but warring with her feeling that the bereaved 'lamb' must be coddled. "Is she ill? Suddenly very, very ill?" asked Claudia, clearly thinking this could be the only appropriate explanation that she could possibly provide people at the reception.

"I think she's just tired, perhaps," said Myrtle.

Claudia did not seem to be impressed by this explanation. It was obviously, to her, a dereliction of duty. She pursed her lips closed and continued scrubbing at a stubborn spot on the counter.

Myrtle was then tasked with setting out serving pieces. She delved into drawers and cabinets. "Wow. Josie does have a lot of silver," she muttered.

Claudia peered in the cabinet. "It would be nice if we could use some of it. Look how tarnished it is! I wonder if it's ever been polished."

Miles came up behind them and cleared his throat. "I just saw Josie arrive while I was putting out more trash. She walked in another entrance."

Myrtle said, "No worries! I'll be her stand-in for the reception."

Claudia fluffed up a casserole with a slotted spoon. "I wonder if she remembered to give the minister his honorarium," she said grimly. "Poor Dr. Bartleby. It's very sad."

"I won't plan on standing in for *that*," said Myrtle.

The guests were starting to arrive. Claudia manned her station alongside Myrtle and several other women. Claudia said, "Remember that *this* pitcher has sweet tea and this one is unsweetened. And there's also ice water, lemonade, and different soft drinks."

Myrtle listened with half an ear as people came in. She explained that Josie had gone upstairs to rest and then moved on to what the different casseroles were. Or, at least, what she guessed they were. The rhythm in the kitchen was a complete dance of moving aside empty casserole dishes to someone washing them, replacing them with new casseroles, and serving.

She was also keeping an eye out for suspects. When she spotted Cady coming in she made the high sign to Miles. He frowned, and then saw Cady. With a resigned look on his face he followed her into the large living room next to the kitchen.

The rest of the reception was something of a blur to Myrtle. She wished she'd thought this morning to put her comfortable shoes on. Because of the funeral dress disaster, she'd decided to put her nicer shoes on instead and dress up the fact that she was wearing slacks. As she shifted from foot to foot on the hard tiled floor, she was sorely rueing that decision.

She was so busy contemplating her sore feet that when a rodent-like face zoomed in front of hers she gasped and automatically brandished a serving spoon in front of her. Then she realized who was in front of her. "Oh, Erma. It's you."

"Had to pay my respects to Janie," she said. "Say, Myrtle, can you give me an extra helping of that hash brown casserole?" Her eyes lit up greedily as Myrtle sighed and helped her to another scoop.

"It's Josie," said Myrtle sternly.

Erma suddenly peered in alarm around her. "Uh ...just wondering what you brought in, Myrtle. You know, so I can keep an eye out for it."

Myrtle knit her brows. "Why? Do you think it might leap out at you from a dark corner?"

Erma flushed a blotchy red. "Course not! Because I want to sample it, naturally. Because your cooking is always so ... good."

One of the church ladies made a choking sound beside her. Myrtle staunchly ignored her.

"As a matter of fact, I was a little low on funeral foods at home. Miles and I are making a run to the store this afternoon. We brought some granola bars."

More coughing next to her.

Erma gave a crooked smile. "Nice idea. Why not? Sometimes people gotta eat and run, you know? May as well bring something they can grab and go with. Have you seen Miles?" she asked abruptly with a gleam in her eye.

"I think he's talking to someone. About something," said Myrtle impatiently. There was a line growing behind Erma and Myrtle was ready to be done.

"Well I saw him through the door there as I was waiting in line." Erma's eyes grew large. "He's talking to Veronica. That young girl. Miles is a dark horse, isn't he? But Myrtle, don't worry. Men may stray temporarily, but they always end up realizing older is better."

Myrtle gave her a cross look. "Miles and I are *not* a couple. We're friends who fight crime together. And Veronica is *not* a young girl."

"Of course she is!" Erma snorted. She turned and craned her head to look through the door to the living room. She reached across the counter and grabbed Myrtle's arm. "Look! You can see them together."

Claudia bellowed behind Myrtle. "Ladies! No nitter-nattering in the line, please! Mourning mouths to feed!" She swept away to handle the developing crisis of someone returning to the line for seconds before everyone had had firsts.

Myrtle yanked her arm away from Erma, brushing her sleeve absently, and peered through the doorway. "For heaven's sake, Erma. That's not Veronica at all! That's Cady Flosser."

Erma frowned. "Cady? I thought her name was Veronica."

"There *is* a Veronica, but she's not this girl. And Miles has no interest in Cady whatsoever."

Erma was, as usual, not listening. She was already somewhere else in her mind. "Hey, maybe you can still do a write-up on my trip, Myrtle. The vacation I went on to the lake? You don't *have* to use pictures. You could just write up little snippets of my trip. Make it real peppy and cute."

Myrtle, who was not feeling peppy and cute, gestured down the serving line with her spoon. "Erma, I can't talk right now. Hungry mouths. Get yourself some sweet tea or a soft drink or something."

"You could even make a real catchy headline. Like: *Erma Sherman Jumps in a Lake!*"

"Now!" growled Myrtle.

CHAPTER SEVENTEEN

IT SEEMED AS THOUGH the entire town of Bradley was at this funeral reception. But Myrtle wasn't surprised. The house was excessively large by Bradley standards and many residents had probably never been inside. If you added the element of curiosity and the fact that most of the town had at least a passing acquaintance with Josie from the library, it was easy to see why the turnout was so large.

Finally the line of people abated and Myrtle had the opportunity to help with the clearing up before heading off with determination to find Miles and see how his interview with Cady had gone. To her surprise, she saw him still sitting with her in the large living room. Erma gave her a sympathetic moue which made her blood pressure creep up.

The living room was packed with people holding plates and glasses and perching on various sofas, chairs, and even gingerly on the sturdier tables. It was a big room with a lot of furniture in it, all from different time periods. There were no places to sit, but when Myrtle gave her encore performance of "the frail old lady," another gentleman hopped immediately up and offered his chair to her. She took it.

"Miss Myrtle!" said Cady, beaming at her. Then she looked slightly abashed. "I suppose I shouldn't be this cheerful. It's a funeral, after all."

"No, dear, it's a funeral *reception*. And those frequently get lively," said Myrtle.

Cady smiled at her. "Miles and I were just talking about engineering. I took a few engineering classes in high school before I decided to focus on the arts."

"Is that so?" asked Myrtle sweetly. But she gave Miles a sour look when Cady wasn't watching. He was *supposed* to be asking her about Roscoe's murder, not about engineering, for heaven's sake.

Miles colored a bit. "When I start talking about engineering, I suppose I can get carried away. Sorry, Cady."

Cady's eyes twinkled at him. "Oh no, I *loved* it. Part of me really misses engineering. The organization, the planning. The math."

"How did you end up at the theater? It seems most *disorganized* and sort of haphazard," said Myrtle. "And there's not much math to be seen outside the ticket booth." She was hoping now to segue into Roscoe's death, although she wasn't exactly sure how she was going to do it from here.

"I was dating someone who was involved in a community theater. It was in a different town. Once I started hanging at that theater, I caught the bug," said Cady ruefully.

Miles said, "You should watch yourself at this particular theater. It might have been safer to stick with engineering."

He was sounding positively avuncular. Myrtle decided he really did need to spend some time with his grandchildren. She would have to figure out how to make that happen.

At least Miles was able to move the subject over to murder. Cady's eyelashes lowered over her large eyes. "That's for sure. I can't believe what happened to Roscoe. He was a nice guy—always nice to me, anyway. He totally *got* my sudden obsession with the theater because he'd been the same way. That was why, I guess, he married Josie to start off with. Her money meant he could spend more time learning his lines and just hanging out in a theater."

Cady seemed to suddenly realize that she was in Josie's house. She put her hand over her mouth and glanced around her.

Myrtle said, "Don't worry, she's not here. She's upstairs, resting."

Cady said bitterly, "Why? Because killing Roscoe was so exhausting?"

This time people sitting around them shot Cady disapproving looks.

Myrtle said in a low voice, "So you think Josie is responsible?"

"Naturally. All of us do. She was the one who got so crazy over what she thought Roscoe was doing with Nandina. She probably killed both of them," Cady's voice was scornful.

Myrtle said, "I've heard cast members mention that Josie seems suspicious. But I've also heard them talking about Skip."

Cady raised her eyebrows, seemingly genuinely surprised by this. "Skip? Why would Skip kill Roscoe? That doesn't even make any sense."

"I guess because Roscoe knew that Skip had killed Nandina. Maybe Roscoe was trying to blackmail Skip and get some extra money. We all know that Josie was the one with the money. Maybe they met up so that Skip could pay Roscoe and Skip killed him instead of paying him," said Myrtle.

Cady shook her head and looked worried. "I can't see Skip killing anyone. Can you? He's got a poet's heart. Oh, maybe in a fit of passion. I could *maybe* see him murdering Nandina because he felt if *he* couldn't have her then *no one* could. Some sort of romantic passion like that. But I can't see him being cold and calculating and planning to meet up with Roscoe and murder him at the theater." Cady was quiet for a moment and then said sharply, "Who said that Skip did it?"

"A couple of people. Blaine mentioned that there was evidence that Skip returned to the theater. And then Veronica mentioned that she was leaving the theater after doing some work on sets and she saw Skip coming into the theater. She said that was unusual for him," said Myrtle.

"What's unusual is Veronica going to the theater night before last. There was *nothing* wrong with those sets. I know because I worked on them earlier, myself. If that was her excuse, she had other reasons for being at the theater. Maybe *she* killed Roscoe because he knew something about *her* killing Nandina," said Cady. "When I think I used to look up to Veronica, it makes me sick!"

Myrtle said abruptly, "Someone told me that you were seen coming out of Mr. Toucan's office recently looking guilty. It was wondered whether you'd had anything to do with the message that was posted on social media the day of Nandina's murder."

Now Cady looked seriously baffled. "What? No. I don't know what you're talking about, anyway. There was something posted on social media when Nandina was murdered?"

"A Twitter update. Something to do with the *better off dead Nandina Marshall,*" said Myrtle.

"This is the first I heard about it," said Cady, shaking her head.

"What about the other part? Were you ever coming out of Mr. Toucan's office looking guilty?" asked Myrtle.

Cady was quiet for a few moments. "I think I might know what that's about. But it was way before the murder, so I don't see how it ties in. I was just coming into the front door of the theater. Mr. Toucan likes to leave the lights off unless there's a production—you know, to save on his electric bill. It was dark, I was quiet. And I saw Veronica coming out of Mr. Toucan's office. She had money in her hand."

Miles said, "You said it was dark. Are you sure it was Veronica?"

"Positive," said Cady.

Myrtle said, "Couldn't she have had a good explanation for coming out of Mr. Toucan's office? I know she did a lot of work at the theater after hours."

"She's no accountant," said Cady with a laugh. "No, there was no reason for her to be coming out of there. Especially holding money. She didn't see me, but I waited a minute or two after she left in the direction of the stage before I went into Mr. Toucan's office. I'm real familiar with the way the room is because I do a lot of stuff in there with the programs and all. His cash box wasn't where it usually is."

"When I've been over to Mr. Toucan's theater," said Myrtle, "Tidiness and organization aren't two words that come to mind. And my incompetent housekeeper allegedly cleans for him, so that wouldn't help things, either. How do you know the cash box was moved?"

Cady was becoming impatient. "Because I put the cash box in a particular spot, myself! I help Mr. Toucan out with accounting. He's terrible with figures. I know it was moved. No one else had been in there but Veronica."

Miles said, "Why didn't you tell someone? Mr. Toucan? Or even the police?"

"I didn't want to think it was true," said Cady sadly. "It was hero worship, I guess. I convinced myself that maybe she had some sort of business with Mr. Toucan. Paying for more set equipment or something. But I knew, deep down, that wasn't true. It made *me* feel guilty because I knew Mr. Toucan doesn't have much money and because I love the theater and want it to be a success. So I walked out of the office and, yeah, my face probably looked guilty. I ran into *her*," said Cady, gesturing to Erma across the room. "Mr. Toucan's friend. But I had nothing to do with anything missing from his office, no matter what anyone says."

"What were you doing the night Roscoe died?" asked Myrtle. "I know sometimes you come back late at night. Did you happen to see anything when you were going past the theater?"

"Nothing. I didn't even drive by there. I was so tired that I took a shortcut home and went straight to bed." She hesitated. "Hey, you don't think I had anything to do with this, do you? You know I didn't kill Nandina. And I liked Roscoe. He was a nice guy."

"Oh no, no. We're asking everyone if they might have seen or heard something, that's all. All right, so just some gut feelings here, right? Veronica and Josie seem likely suspects to you?" asked Myrtle briskly.

Cady looked relieved that she wasn't a suspect. "Yes. And, okay, maybe throw Blaine in there, too. Although he's really just too good-looking to look like a killer to me. If he said that Skip left something, that's kind of weird. Skip is very particular about his stuff. I can't see him leaving his things scattered everywhere. He has personal space issues with his belongings—might as well have a *keep out* sign on them at the theater."

Myrtle nodded. "Okay, thanks. And if you think of anything else, just give me a call. I'm in the phone book."

Cady grinned at her. "You mean online. People still use phone books?" And then, "Okay, well, it was good talking with both of you. I'm going to pick up a little more food on the way out ... to go. That way I don't have to worry about supper."

Miles and Myrtle watched her go. Then Myrtle's gaze wandered to the other side of the room before she abruptly jerked it back. "Ugh!"

"What's wrong?" asked Miles, trying to follow the direction she'd been looking in. He frowned and then said, "Ugh."

"I wish I could un-see that," muttered Myrtle. "The idea of Erma and Mr. Toucan together is rather disturbing somehow."

"The idea of Erma with *anyone* is rather disturbing," said Miles.

"Now I know why Erma was here. It was obvious she didn't know who Josie even was," said Myrtle. "It's not as if she goes to the library. Annoying woman."

"She might have known Roscoe, though, if she spent a lot of time with Mr. Toucan," said Miles.

Myrtle shuddered. "Let's get out of here. We still need to get to the store."

A nasal voice called behind her, "Remember, Myrtle! Little teasers about my vacation on *Bugle* social media!"

Myrtle walked faster.

"I'm assuming that we're going to the grocery store now," said Miles. "Since the granola bars had originally figured into my supper plan and now they're staying in Josie's kitchen."

They were outside Josie's house and Miles was unlocking his car.

"I was hoping that Josie would come running outside," grumbled Myrtle. "That she would tell me how happy she was that I filled in for her and that she felt rejuvenated after her rest. Then she could tell me what happened the night Roscoe died."

"You're not listening again," observed Miles. "But I will say that every part of that last statement of yours was completely unlikely. Josie is probably up in her room with a large drink. She looked unnerved at the funeral."

"I suppose so," said Myrtle. And then she added, "When did you want to go to the store? Were we going there this afternoon?"

Miles gripped the steering wheel and took a deep, steadying breath. "As a matter of fact, we should probably go there now."

"Good. I didn't have anything to eat at the reception and I'm starving. I'm not in the mood to try to figure out a meal out of a can of diced tomatoes and creamed corn."

Miles said, "What did you think of our conversation with Cady?"

"About Josie? That was to be expected. I'm sure most of the cast probably thinks that she was responsible. I haven't heard anyone speak fond words about Josie. They're probably *hoping* it's her because she's not directly involved with the theater. But I was a little surprised that she was so sour about Veronica."

"I know. I'd thought at first that she looked up to Veronica as a mentor. But it sounds like she's gotten upset about her," said Miles, pulling into the grocery store parking lot.

"It sounded more like she was protecting Skip. She jumped to his defense."

They got out of the car. Miles looked ahead and said, "Isn't that Skip there? Going into the store?"

"It sure is. Perfect! We can knock out two birds with one stone," said Myrtle, grabbing her cane and hurrying toward the store.

They got two carts and headed in.

"Do you have your list this time?" asked Miles.

"The list? I think so. I think it's at the bottom of my pocketbook." Myrtle put her purse in the cart and started pulling things out of it. There were entirely too many bits of paper and loyalty cards in the purse. "Where on earth did I put it?"

"It should be pretty easy for you to shop. You need *everything*," said Miles.

"So do you!"

"Just follow my lead. I did make sure to put my grocery list in my pocket this morning." And, reaching into the pocket of his navy jacket, he pulled out a neatly folded piece of paper.

Myrtle leaned toward him to peer at the paper. "And the items on your list are in order of the actual rows in the store. Impressive. But I'm not sure I need exactly the things that you do. I have no need for hand sanitizer, for one."

"You should reconsider that," said Miles as they walked toward the produce section. "Think of all the hands you shook this morning at the funeral. I must have washed my hands six or seven times today."

"Maybe you shook hands. I didn't shake a single one. People don't shake octogenarian ladies' hands. They hug them."

"Even worse," said Miles with a shudder.

"Now where's that Skip? I want to make sure that he's got a cart and is doing a *real* shopping trip. If he's running in for just the one item, we need to waylay him now before he leaves."

"That's him there," said Miles, gesturing to the deli counter.

"I do believe I need some sliced ham and Swiss cheese for sandwiches," said Myrtle, pushing her cart toward the young man.

He was looking at his phone as they pulled up beside them. When he saw who it was, he put his phone away and gave them a crooked smile. "Here to buy more squash?" he asked.

Myrtle laughed. "No, just everything else on my list. I've been so busy that I haven't had time to get to the store."

Skip nodded. "Were you at the funeral this morning?"

"We were. Very soggy out. Thankfully, it seems as if it's stopped now." As Myrtle said this, there was a peal of thunder and she sighed.

Skip said, almost as if he were speaking to himself, "The whole thing was just wrong."

"What was?" asked Miles.

"Everything. Roscoe being dead. The fact that Josie had the chance to play the grieving widow. Winnie showing up like that and making a big scene." Skip shook his head.

Myrtle said, cautiously, "I was talking to some of the cast members and they were saying that they thought you might have been at the theater the night of Roscoe's death. Your car was seen going in. And then it was mentioned that maybe you accidentally left something at the theater that night."

Skip's eyes narrowed. "Let me guess. Veronica."

Myrtle gazed back at him steadily. "Let's just say that it was *someone*."

"I wasn't there. I don't go hang out at the theater at night like the other cast members. If there's no performance, I'm not there. I did drive downtown, but I didn't go to the theater, I went to pick up a late-night burger before the fast food place closed. A man can't live on squash alone," he said with a wink. "Fortunately, I had a couple of dollars in my glove compartment, since I realized in the drive-through that I didn't have my wallet with me."

"You left it at the theater?" asked Miles.

"No. I know I didn't leave my wallet at the theater. It's just not the kind of thing that I do. I don't trail my belongings behind me like a comet," said Skip.

"Then why was it there?" asked Myrtle.

"I think someone was trying to set me up," said Skip. "Clearly. And I think that someone is probably Josie."

"Josie? How would she have gotten hold of your wallet?" asked Myrtle.

"It would be pretty easy for someone who is actively looking for a way to set someone up. We all leave our personal belongings in the dressing room when we practice on stage. While we were all practicing, she could have slipped in there, found my wallet, and made sure it was near the scene of the crime." The deli worker handed Skip his order of roast beef. "And, let's face it. Josie had the biggest reason for wanting to get rid of Roscoe. She was furious with him," said Skip.

Myrtle nodded. "I'm just not sure that such a *planned* murder fits with Josie's motive. It seems like it would be more spontaneous. More of a crime of passion."

Skip shrugged. "But her personality is that of a planner. Maybe she's not passionate enough to carry out a crime of passion, but she still wanted him gone. And didn't want to go to jail for it." He looked at his watch. "And now, if you'll excuse me? I need to finish up my shopping."

Miles and Myrtle moved through the produce section slowly. Myrtle absently picked up a bunch of bananas. "I just don't see Josie setting Skip up. I just don't."

Miles said, "Maybe Skip is right, though. Maybe she's a planner. Maybe it *wasn't* a crime of passion. Maybe it was a crime of revenge. Josie wanted revenge on Roscoe for embarrassing her."

Myrtle shook her head and reached for a honeydew melon. "I don't see it," she repeated. "Remember the state of her kitchen? Remember Drill Instructor Claudia whipping it into shape? That was not the kitchen of a planner. It was the kitchen of someone who's caught up in chaos. I don't see her having the fortitude to strategically plan out Roscoe's murder and pin it on someone else."

"Who *do* you see?"

"Veronica maybe. She seems more calculating. She's certainly a very self-aware woman. Remember how she always poses for your pictures?" asked Myrtle.

Miles made a face. "Yes. I have a slew of pictures that I need to delete off my phone. Or get Jack to delete off my phone. Unless you need them for your story?"

"If there are any that don't have your finger in them, I would like them. Who knows? Sloan is always saying our stories need to have a little visual interest. I think he likes more photos for the online version of the paper, too," said Myrtle.

"It'll be especially interesting if Veronica ends up being the murderer," murmured Miles. "What did you think about Cady's story about Veronica taking cash out of Mr. Toucan's office?"

Myrtle said, "I think it's very interesting. It makes me wonder if that were something of a habit of hers. What if her pilfering was a reason why Mr. Toucan was suffering financial straits?"

"Wouldn't he notice the money was gone?" asked Miles.

"Not necessarily. His office isn't very organized and I don't think he's a wizard with accounting. If Veronica took small enough amounts, sort of a petty cash thing, he'd probably never even notice," said Myrtle. "And if Cady saw Veronica in the act of stealing, maybe Nandina did, too. And we know what that means."

"Blackmail," said Miles. "At least, that appears to be Nandina's usual m.o."

"Although, I somehow can't see Veronica strangling Nandina," said Myrtle. "And I can't really see her striking Roscoe and pushing him down a staircase, either. I can definitely see her slipping sleeping pills in Nandina's wine, though."

Miles said, "I think she's tough as nails. I don't think she'd have had a problem in the world killing either one of them."

Myrtle said, "I'm wondering about Veronica and Blaine and all the time they spend together at the theater. I know they love acting and all, but I'm wondering if they don't have an ulterior motive for hanging out there at night."

Miles raised his eyebrows as they headed toward aisle one. "You think they're having an affair?"

"Why not? Cady said that Veronica's pretense for being at the theater was completely fabricated. That made Cady believe Veronica was responsible for killing Roscoe, but might it also mean that she and Blaine were meeting at the theater secretly. After all, Mr. Toucan said that Blaine spends a lot of time at the theater studying his lines and writing," said Myrtle. "Unless the reason Veronica was there was to have more opportunity to swipe cash from the cash box."

"I don't know. I haven't seen or heard any evidence that they were a couple. I think it's just your favorite pastime, putting couples together. So far we've had Blaine paired with Nandina, Cady, and now Veronica. Isn't that just your imagination working overtime?" asked Miles.

"Maybe. But I'm not so sure. I know one thing. Mr. Toucan is worried sick about what this means for his theater," said Myrtle.

"He should be. It's a very costly endeavor, even when there *aren't* murders at your business and when there *aren't* staffing problems because your cast is getting murdered one by one. The licensing fees themselves must be tremendous," said Miles.

"What licensing fees?"

"Well, to put on a production, you need to buy a script. Not really buy it, I guess. More like pay a licensing fee and royalty fees so that you can put the production on," said Miles.

"You mean he had to *pay* somebody to be able to put on that dreadful *Malaise*? I've never heard of it before," said Myrtle.

"Maybe that's why he chose it. Because it was unknown and would have been cheap," said Miles with a shrug.

"Hmm." This line of thought seemed to jog something in Myrtle's brain but she couldn't seem to figure out what.

Miles gave her a sideways glance as they passed the salad dressing. "You know, you need to take the afternoon off. You looked uncomfortable when we were leaving the reception."

"It was just Josie's awful stone tile floors. They killed my feet," said Myrtle.

"And now here you are canvassing a grocery store to stock up your pantry," said Miles. "As I said, just take the afternoon off. Put your feet up for a while. Stare mindlessly at the lake."

"If it's not thundering and raining," muttered Myrtle. But she had to admit, after the busy morning Miles's idea held some appeal.

CHAPTER EIGHTEEN

BY LATE AFTERNOON AND after unloading the bags of groceries, Myrtle had to admit that Miles was right. Her feet were telling her she should sit down for a while. And ever since Miles had mentioned the lake, it had made her want to go outside and enjoy it. She had a rocking chair on the dock where her yard rolled down to the water. She'd long since given the boat to Red and his family, but she still liked to sit on the dock and feel the breeze and watch the boats on the lake.

Myrtle took a towel to sit on since it had been a rainy morning, a pair of sunglasses, slipped her cell phone into her pants pocket, and made her way down the hill to the dock. The rain had finally stopped and the air smelled fresh. She put the towel on the seat of the rocking chair and plopped down.

There weren't as many boaters out as there would usually be. She saw Gordon Millford fishing in the middle of the lake and waved at him. A few minutes later there was a lone boat with a boy water-skiing behind it and whooping it up. Then she spotted a third boat after a while. It held a couple who seemed very engrossed with each other. She squinted at the boat. She saw the sun glinting off the woman's red hair. Her companion had blond, curly hair. Myrtle could have sworn they were Blaine and Veronica.

She didn't want to go back up to the house and find her binoculars. By the time she did, the boat would likely be long gone, even as slow as it was going. So Myrtle opened her cell phone to the camera and zoomed in as far as the device would let her go. Although the resulting image was a bit blurry, it was clear—it was Blaine and Veronica.

She dialed Miles. "Miles?" she asked excitedly.

Miles sounded as if he might have been enjoying a late-afternoon nap. "Mmm?"

"Blaine and Veronica! I'm seeing them together right now! I'm sitting by the lake and they're together in a boat."

Miles asked groggily, "Together? So, are they just sitting and talking? Because that's kind of a coincidence if they're suddenly in a relationship when we were just talking about that."

"Maybe it's a coincidence, but it makes sense that they wouldn't want to be seen together in town where everyone would talk. They'd have more privacy on a boat. Maybe they didn't want everyone to know that they're a couple," said Myrtle.

"But are you *sure* they're a couple? Could they just be two cast members talking about their really bad week?" asked Miles.

Myrtle took her phone away from her ear and zoomed in once again with her camera in time to see Blaine give Veronica a light kiss on the mouth. Veronica turned away.

"Oh, they're definitely a couple," she said. "At least, Blaine seems to think they are."

"Okay. Although I'm not sure it really changes anything. So they're having a relationship. Big deal. They're both attractive people working with each other. It happens," said Miles.

"Does this mean that Blaine was involved with both Nandina *and* Veronica? Or is this a recent development?" mused Myrtle.

Miles said in a sleepy voice, "I don't know. But can we talk about it tomorrow? I thought we were calling a moratorium on investigating for the rest of the day. I'm planning on resuming my nap, having a simple supper, and turning in early."

"Sounds like a recipe for a night of full-blown insomnia," said Myrtle with a sniff. It was always most aggravating when one's sidekick refused to play along. "Be sure and come by for a coffee tonight if you find you can't sleep. We can kick around who the killer might be."

Blaine and Veronica were out of sight now, but Myrtle continued staring out at the water. Blaine and Veronica. Nights working at the theater. Veronica and junk mail. Then she called Mr. Toucan.

"Myrtle? Hi, how are you. It's been a long day, hasn't it?"

Mr. Toucan did sound very tired. But then, perhaps it was just that Erma Sherman was wearing on him.

"It certainly has been. I'd imagine it would be very emotional for you having to go to the funeral of a second cast member. Did you go home afterward and rest for a while?" asked Myrtle.

"No, I needed to go back to the theater and work on my accounting books," said Mr. Toucan with a sigh. "Can't seem to get the numbers to do what they're supposed to. Very distressing. But I'm home now. I decided to take the books home with me and try to figure them out from here. Although I'm afraid they don't seem to make any more sense at home."

"Mr. Toucan, I was wondering about the plays you're putting on."

"The plays, yes," said Mr. Toucan in a slightly slurred voice.

Myrtle wondered if he'd perhaps dipped into the cooking sherry.

"Yes. I was talking with someone recently ... just chatting, you know ... and he mentioned how expensive it is to put on plays," said Myrtle.

"Oh goodness, yes. The sets, the costumes. The utilities. Oh, the utility issues we're running into are absolutely heinous!" More slurring. "I need to find ways to reduce costs. I'm thinking about borrowing most of the set pieces for my next production."

"I'm sure. But I was wondering more about the actual scripts. The licensing fees or royalties, perhaps. Something like that."

Mr. Toucan groaned. "Yes! It's highway robbery, that's what it is. Highway robbery, I tell you. Even for plays that no one has heard of at all."

"Plays like *Malaise*?" asked Myrtle.

"Yes! Actually ... no. Not like *Malaise*. I got lucky with *Malaise* because there were no costs at all. And, considering all the work I've been doing around the theater, I really needed that buffer."

Myrtle said, "And the reason that there's no fee for *Malaise*—is that because someone you knew wrote it? A friend of the theater? Someone like Blaine?"

"That's it precisely!" said Mr. Toucan excitedly. "He wrote the play and said he was just happy to have the exposure. A credit list on his resume."

Myrtle sat very still. "Mr. Toucan, I was wondering how that process went. Did he just bring you a completed play?"

"He did. Oh, it was months ago. But then it ended up still being a work-in-progress." Mr. Toucan gave a tipsy laugh. "As a matter of fact, I think that he's *still* working on it now! He's always tweaking it."

"Do you remember any of the tweaks he's made along the way?" asked Myrtle intently.

"Some big things. Some little things. It was a very organic process. I think he was trying to write a part that would be suitable for Veronica. But Nandina, bless her, had put some pressure on for him to have her play a larger role. I think it must be very hard to be a playwright," said Mr. Toucan.

"What about the scene with Nandina on the bed? Was that in the original version of the play?" asked Myrtle.

"I—well, I can't remember," admitted Mr. Toucan. "You'd have to look at the original draft."

"I'd like that," said Myrtle. "I'd very much like that. Is it possible that I could go over there now?"

"Now?" he squeaked. "I don't think anyone is over there now."

"Just the same, I'd really like to see the drafts. I have a few questions and a look at the original documents would be very helpful for me."

"I suppose you could let yourself in the back door," said Mr. Toucan doubtfully. "There's a lockbox on the door with a key in it. We have a lot of cast members coming and going, so it's better if people have access. The code is 5872."

Myrtle carefully made a note on her phone. "Thank you. I don't think I'll be there for very long. Do you have any idea where the drafts might be?"

"A guess is downstairs where the dressing area is. I don't think it's in my office. Blaine spent so much time handing the script back and forth that I finally just surrendered the approval process to him completely. Told him I trusted him to come up with a good play for the company. And I was getting it for free, after all, so everything I made was pure profit," said Mr. Toucan.

Myrtle asked, "By the way, do you know of any reason why Veronica might need to deal with money or accounting in your office?"

Mr. Toucan gave a rather high-pitched laugh. "Veronica? Certainly not. She doesn't have a head for figures at all. In fact, I don't think she handles her *own* finances very well."

"Got it. Okay, thanks. I'll talk to you later," she said.

Myrtle sat staring out at the lake. She stared for long enough that she saw Blaine and Veronica pass by again and head back to his small house on the lake front. This time Blaine spotted her and raised a hand to wave. Veronica still seemed as if she was leaning away from Blaine somehow. Myrtle waved back and then stood up from the rocking chair with the help of her cane. It may mean nothing if Blaine changed the script dramatically in terms of Nandina. Red would certainly not take such a change as hard evidence. But it was influential evidence, surely. It wouldn't just be a retired English teacher pointing out differences between draft one and draft two. Myrtle fully expected to take the drafts with her. It wasn't as if they were in Blaine's *house*. They were in a theater that she'd been given permission and even a code to enter. It should still be admissible.

It may not mean much in a court of law. But just the same, Myrtle decided she would go to the theater and search for those drafts while Blaine was safely out on the lake. Just in case. For half a second she entertained the thought of taking Miles with her. But then she remembered his nap and decided to just loop him in later. Sidekicks needed sleep too.

She'd walked back up to the house and grabbed an empty grocery bag to bring the drafts home in. As Myrtle walked out her front door, she gasped. There was a large tote bag filled to the brim with squash. "Wanda must be stopped!" she muttered. She spotted a bit of torn paper taped to the bag. It said: *Mertel. Thanx for helpin.*

It was all very kind hearted of Wanda. But really.

Unfortunately, she'd been raised in a similar manner to Miles. There was something in her that refused to throw away food. She could still hear her mother's voice from long-ago: *remember the starving children in …* wherever they were starving at the time. With a sigh she hoisted the tote bag up on her shoulder, tested her balance and bore down a bit more on the cane, and set off for the theater. If *they* disposed of it, at least she wouldn't be around to witness it.

When Myrtle got to the theater, she climbed the steps in the back, set down the bag of squash, and entered the code to get in.

"Hello?" she called out. No one answered. The last thing she wanted to do was to have someone surprise her in the dark.

Myrtle felt along the interior wall for a light switch, fumbled a switch on, and saw light dimly illuminate the backstage area. She set the squash down on a small table and glanced around her. No, this didn't seem to be an area where there would be a bunch of papers. There were poles around that Myrtle guessed were used to push set pieces around during scene changes. The bed from Nandina's fatal scene was on a small, castered platform. The living room set was also there. It was cramped and seemed limited to what was needed for each performance.

Myrtle next found a light switch and a set of stairs that she guessed led to the dressing area downstairs that Mr. Toucan had mentioned on the phone. She walked down the creaky wooden stairs and entered a large, dark room. Once again she fumbled with lights. This time the room was illuminated brilliantly.

It was somewhat creepy when deserted. Myrtle shivered. There were mirrors everywhere: full length, tabletop, and wall-length. Costumes hung here and there and there was makeup scattered on a long table in front of the mirrored wall. There were also a couple of bags of overripe squash. Myrtle made a face.

Across the room was what looked like a small lounge area with two folding chairs and an armchair next to an end table. The end table had a couple of drawers in it and was the only place Myrtle could conceive that a draft might be. She sat in the threadbare armchair and opened the drawers.

Bingo. The bottom drawer held a script with lots of markings on it. Myrtle pulled her glasses out of her pocketbook and started reading.

A few minutes later, she got to the part in the play where Nandina died. She nodded her head slowly. As she'd thought. The original version of the play had no scene with Nandina sleeping. In fact, the original version of *Malaise* didn't have Nandina in the scene at all. Veronica, Skip, and Blaine were to be discussing life in the living room, instead. Written on the back of one of the printed pages was the new scene—the one in which Nandina lost her life.

Myrtle held the pages tightly and stood up to return upstairs. She had what she'd wanted. Red should be very interested to see this.

She turned the lights off behind her and slowly ascended the stairs to the backstage area.

"Miss Myrtle," said a deep voice. "What a surprise to see you here!"

CHAPTER NINETEEN

BLAINE STEPPED OUT from behind the curtain. His smile was pleasant ... until he saw the papers in Myrtle's hand.

"Why have you got my script, Miss Myrtle?" asked Blaine in a very even voice. He took a couple of steps closer to her and Myrtle casually took a few back until she had a hand leaning on the table she'd put the bag of squash on, for balance.

"What—these papers?" asked Myrtle, looking down at her hands as if surprised to see them there. "Mr. Toucan and I were talking on the phone and when I mentioned I was going downtown, he asked if I could run by the theater and pick up some things for him."

"Like my old script?" asked Blaine, raising an eyebrow. "He didn't want something from his office instead? That seems odd, doesn't it?"

"Does it?" asked Myrtle brightly. She pushed her hand slowly backward until it connected with something solid.

"Nice try, Miss Myrtle. And my hat's off to you. It was stupid of me not to destroy that draft. I'd just assumed that no one would think much about the play itself. Art, you know. It so frequently goes unnoticed." Blaine took another menacing step forward.

Myrtle quickly said, "Why did you do it, Blaine? Did Nandina not want to break up with you?" she studied Blaine's face thoughtfully. "No, that's not it, is it? It was Veronica. Veronica wanted Nandina out of the way. You two were already a couple, although no one knew it. Nandina was pushing Veronica out of all the roles she wanted. She represented a threat to Veronica."

Blaine laughed. "You've got a very simple view of the universe, Miss Myrtle. You think that I would kill over Veronica's pique over losing roles?"

"I don't think that's all of it, no." Myrtle took a deep breath and decided to go out on a limb. "But I think you were devoted to Veronica. And when she told you that Nandina was blackmailing her over stealing petty cash from Mr. Toucan, you took it upon yourself to eliminate the problem for her. In the hopes that she would end up caring for you as much as you care for her."

The smile left Blaine's face and now he appeared displeased. "She was upset. I took care of it. Problem solved."

Myrtle remembered the scene on the boat earlier. The body language told a story. A story that Blaine was feeling a lot more amorous than distant Veronica was. She said slowly, confidence gradually making her voice stronger, "Veronica never actually asked you to murder Nandina, did she? She must have been horrified that you'd do such a thing on her behalf. She's a thief, not a killer. But you took her unhappiness as a directive. Without her guidance."

"So she's a little ungrateful." Blaine shrugged. "She'll come around eventually. She was just surprised, that's all."

"More than surprised. I believe Veronica was merely playing a prank. I overheard Cady saying that Veronica played pranks on people—one time signing somebody up for every junk mail list she could find. Veronica slipped sleeping pills in Nandina's drink ... right? She probably told you about it. I can just see her now: *wouldn't it be funny if Nandina was too sleepy to act?* But you took it farther. You told Veronica you were going to change the script to make a scene where Nandina was in a bed. Even better! Nandina would be very drowsy, would be in the set bed, and then she'd look really foolish and unprofessional. What Veronica didn't know is that you were planning on quickly finishing her off during the set change. You changed the script to make it easier for yourself."

"What's another script change?" asked Blaine with a twisted smile. "I was making changes all along—why not another?" Blaine almost casually picked up a lashing used for set changes. Myrtle's throat constricted when she saw it, but she was determined to remain calm. She needed to rely on her wits to get out of this.

"It all went smoothly, too. Although the social media post was a bit catty and risky. Veronica again, I'm guessing?"

"She couldn't resist," said Blaine with a sigh. His face was impassive as he moved closer to Myrtle. "But then, she didn't realize my plans or else she wouldn't have posted about Nandina being better off dead."

Myrtle swallowed and continued, "Or, at least it all went smoothly until Roscoe revealed he knew something. And wanted money to keep the secret to himself."

"He always seemed like such a nice guy, too," said Blaine.

"What was it that he knew? Had he noticed you were spending too much time at Nandina's 'bedside' during the set change? Had he spotted Veronica slipping something into Nandina's drink before the show? Or had he, maybe, realized that the script had been radically altered to accommodate a murder?" asked Myrtle, holding up the sheaf of papers.

"Who knows? He didn't say. He didn't *have* to say. It was enough that he knew about the murder. And that he was threatening to expose us. I can't let us be exposed," said Blaine, a warning in his voice.

"So you arranged to meet him as he wanted, to talk in private at the theater when no one else was in there. You'd already swiped Skip's wallet from the dressing room earlier to plant evidence against him," said Myrtle.

Blaine nodded. "But he was asking for it. Skip can be pretty obnoxious. And he *could* have done it. He just didn't."

"I have a feeling that he also wasn't stalking Nandina, as Veronica had stated. Did she completely fabricate that?" asked Myrtle.

"It certainly helped," said Blaine coolly. "It deflected attention."

"Veronica worked pretty hard to deflect attention," said Myrtle. "But then, she must have been terrified that she would be uncovered as an accomplice to the crimes. She'd have done anything to keep attention away from both of you."

"She definitely had a motive to obfuscate," agreed Blaine with a crooked smile.

"And I thought you were such a nice guy because you were kind to Jack," said Myrtle sadly.

"He's a sweet kid. I'm sorry that he's going to miss his grandma."

Blaine lunged toward Myrtle and she quickly moved behind the little table, shoving it over along with the large bag of squash. Blaine slipped, yelling curses as he went down.

Myrtle's cane was too short to reach him. She grabbed one of the set moving poles and brandished it at him. "Stay back, Blaine," she warned him. "This pole is heavy enough to kill you and I'd rather not. Although I will," she said steadily.

Blaine burst out laughing as he lay on the floor with squash all around him. "I'd like to see you try, old woman."

Myrtle narrowed her eyes. She didn't mind one bit being called an old woman. But being laughed at was something else.

"Blaine?" asked a hesitant voice from behind Blaine. Myrtle squinted through the dimly lit room to see Cady standing there.

Blaine swung his head around.

And that's when Myrtle seized the opportunity to swing the pole and whack Blaine across the shoulders and back of his head. He fell over the squash again and Myrtle yelled to the frozen Cady, "Come on and help me!" Grabbing some of the set lashings, she started tying Blaine up. Cady quickly snapped out of it and Myrtle let her take over while she fumbled for her phone to call Red.

Red sounded groggy. With all the late nights, he must have been getting forty winks. "Wait, *what*?" he asked.

"I said Blaine did it. He killed Nandina and Roscoe. Well, it was mostly Blaine, anyway, even if Veronica isn't entirely blameless, especially after the fact. Such a pity because he *was* nice to Jack. So you probably need to arrest both of them. But arrest Blaine first because Cady and I have him restrained right now backstage at the theater." Myrtle decided that her nerves were making her a bit garrulous.

"I'm on my way," said Red grimly. "And I'll call the state police to bring Veronica in for questioning. Lieutenant Perkins is at the station."

Red came and took Blaine away in handcuffs, asking Myrtle and Cady to stay put so that he could take statements. Cady broke down in tears as Blaine was led away. "I didn't really want to believe it was him," she admitted tearfully. "I used to have the biggest crush on him. And it's Veronica, too?"

Myrtle nodded.

Cady said, "Mr. Toucan is going to flip *out*." But in the next breath, showing the resilience of youth, she said, "But I guess I'll have more roles open to me now."

Considering most of the regular troupe was either murdered or arrested, that sounded very likely to Myrtle.

Red eventually returned with Lt. Perkins: a tall, wiry man with a military haircut and a polite manner. "Who's with Blaine and Veronica then?" asked Cady, looking worried.

"Don't worry," said Red. "They have plenty of officers charged with questioning and booking them at the station. Now let's talk about what *you* know," said Red.

Cady said, "I don't know a whole lot, I'm afraid. I came back to the theater to get rid of the old programs and make sure

someone wouldn't accidentally give them out at a performance."
She made a face. "You know, with Roscoe's name listed as a cast
member. We'd already trashed the ones with Nandina in them,
but I remembered we hadn't for Roscoe's."

Myrtle said wryly, "Now you'll probably have to trash the
whole production."

Cady nodded sadly, "Yeah, I think *Malaise* is done for good.
Anyway," she said as Red gave a small prompting cough, "I came
back to the theater. When I arrived backstage, it was totally obvious to me that Blaine was ready to kill Miss Myrtle."

Myrtle said huffily, "It *should* have been totally obvious that
I was ready to kill *Blaine*."

Cady said quickly, "That too. But—well, I could tell you
were defending yourself, Miss Myrtle. I didn't go, 'Oh, so *Miss
Myrtle* killed Nandina and Roscoe and now is going to kill
Blaine!' That didn't cross my mind."

Lt. Perkins seemed to be struggling with a smile. "So then
you helped Miss Myrtle restrain him."

"No, first she whacked him with that push pole, *then* I
helped her restrain him. But that's about all I know," she said
with a shrug.

"Thanks for giving us your statement," said Perkins. "You're
free to go."

Myrtle said, "And thanks for deciding to help out at the theater tonight. It was a real lifesaver." She winked at Cady who
laughed and gave a wave as she left out the back door of the theater.

"Better have an empty notebook ready," said Red with a sigh. "This account is sure to delve into her soap opera and various local gossip."

Myrtle gave him a squelching look. "Certainly not." She waited until Lt. Perkins had flipped to a new page in his notebook.

"It all started when Miles mentioned licensing and royalty fees. Well, actually, I guess it started when Mr. Toucan had to do some very expensive renovations for the theater. Utility work," explained Myrtle.

Lt. Perkins nodded slowly. "So Mr. Toucan was low on cash."

"I think you'll find Mr. Toucan isn't great at accounting. And he's decidedly low on cash. When Cady mentioned that she'd seen Veronica leaving his office with a handful of money, I wondered if perhaps Veronica had her hand in the till. Mr. Toucan *did* have a lot of expensive repairs. But petty theft certainly wouldn't have helped the situation."

Red said, "And Cady might not have been the only person who caught Veronica in the act."

"Exactly," said Myrtle. "Veronica was unlucky enough to be caught by Nandina. Nandina had a nasty habit of blackmailing people, as we learned from Roscoe."

Lt. Perkins said, "And Veronica complained to Blaine about it."

"I think Veronica complained about a lot of things to Blaine. I think she complained that Nandina was insulting to her. I think she complained that Nandina stole all the good parts. And I think the icing on the cake must have been when

Nandina started blackmailing Veronica. If Mr. Toucan had found out that Veronica had been stealing from him, he would have immediately dropped her from the cast. He likely would have had her arrested. He's serious about his money," said Myrtle.

"So, backing up a little, your friend talked about how expensive the scripts were," said Lt. Perkins. "And this started you thinking about money and the theater."

"Right. And this made me think about *Malaise.* Because I was there on opening night. The play simply wasn't very good. In other words, I had a hard time believing that Mr. Toucan had put a lot of money into acquiring this script."

"What made you decide that Blaine might have written the script?" asked Red.

"Well, Mr. Toucan mentioned that Blaine was a writer. Blaine himself told me that he liked to write while looking out at the lake. Since the play was a bit amateurish, it made me wonder if perhaps it was written by an amateur."

"So you took it upon yourself to confront a crazed killer," said Red dryly. "Why does this not surprise me?"

"Certainly not!" Myrtle gave him a cold look. "I went to the theater to find one of Blaine's old drafts. Mr. Toucan gave me permission to enter the backstage area and even provided me with a key."

"Please continue, Miss Myrtle," said Lt. Perkins. Red sighed.

"I also realized that Blaine and Veronica were a lot friendlier than everyone thought. Or, at least, Blaine was a lot friendlier with Veronica. When I spotted the two of them together in Blaine's boat today, she seemed to be a little distant. From what I could tell. But could you imagine her predicament? If she pushes Blaine away, he might be angry enough to reveal her involvement in the killings."

"What made you think that the two of them might both have been involved?" asked Red. "Just that you saw them together on Blaine's boat?"

"Well, one thing that bothered me was the fact that Nandina had been given sleeping pills and had been strangled. Slipping sleeping pills in a wine glass seems more like a woman's crime to me. And strangulation ... doesn't. Veronica was known as a prankster on the set. Making Nandina perform poorly onstage by slipping pills in her drink sounds like something spiteful she'd have done to get back at Nandina. And there was also that social media message on opening night: *featuring the better off dead Nandina Marshall.* That seemed very catty to me. But hitting a man over the back of the head and shoving him down a staircase seemed a bit more like a man's crime. I started thinking that maybe there were two perpetrators. A man and a woman. Even if Veronica were something of an unwilling partner. She definitely helped cover up the crimes."

Lt. Perkins nodded thoughtfully. "Although others have seemed implicated in the crimes, too."

Myrtle said, "Implicated on purpose, you mean. Especially Skip. Veronica must have been desperate to ensure that no one suspected Blaine—because it meant that her own involvement would be revealed. Veronica impugned Skip's character and made him sound a lot more dangerous than he probably was. She called Skip a stalker. Now, I've no doubt he was smitten with Nandina Marshall. But I bet we'll learn that he never stalked anyone a day in his life. Plus we had Blaine swiping Skip's wallet and then leaving it as 'evidence' that he was at the theater when Roscoe was murdered."

Red said, "I had a point where I was sure that Josie Ragsdale was involved in both murders. Especially after I saw her temper explode at the funeral."

"Josie certainly did seem suspicious. It didn't help that none of the cast liked her. But she didn't seem to be thinking clearly. Her home was a real disaster area, too. It was the cold and calculating part of the murders that just didn't seem to be a fit with Josie's temperament. She seemed more likely to commit a crime of passion," said Myrtle.

A hesitant cough from the door made them turn around. It was Miles, looking abashed. "I heard the sirens," he said. "Is everything all right?"

"It sure is," said Perkins. "Come on in. I know you're half of the crime fighting duo."

"The sleepy half," muttered Myrtle with a sniff. But she smiled at Miles. There had been a moment when she'd wondered if she'd ever see her sidekick again.

Red continued, "Blaine moved toward you in a threatening manner?"

"With a set lashing," said Myrtle, pointing toward the offending item.

Red looked grim.

"In your estimation, he was planning on murdering you to silence you. Is that right?" asked Lt. Perkins.

Miles looked anxiously at the lashing and at Myrtle.

"He most certainly was. At least until he encountered the squash." She gestured again, this time at the copious amount of squash all over the floor. "Wanda had been most insistent that I take it to the theater. Prescient once again."

"Sure am glad you found a practical use for the squash," said Red. "Particularly in light of my squash allergy."

Myrtle said, "Maybe he fell on the squash, but it was the push pole that really finished him off." She turned to the police officers. "Did Blaine squeal on Veronica?"

Red shrugged. "Doesn't really matter if he did or not. She's gone ahead and given us a confession outlining her role in the whole thing ... her theft, Nandina's blackmail, the sleeping pills, her general animosity, the fact that she didn't inform the police when Blaine told her what he'd done. She broke under pressure. She was the motivating factor behind these murders, although she was only directly involved in Nandina's since she put some of her own sleeping pills in Nandina's wine before the curtain went up."

Myrtle said, "Nandina wasn't exactly innocent, either. Remember how she was taunting Veronica in the diner? She knew exactly how to get under Veronica's skin. And she found out that it's always dangerous to blackmail someone."

There was a hesitant knock at the back door. Mr. Toucan stuck his head around. "Okay if I come in?"

Red said, "Sure. I think we're about done here."

Mr. Toucan said anxiously, "Miss Myrtle, are you all right? I was so horrified to hear the news! Cady just texted me and I walked right over."

Walked. Myrtle had been correct about the sherry. "I'm fine, Mr. Toucan. Just ready to have a quiet evening, that's all."

He nodded. "I can't believe this is happening. Blaine and Veronica! My best stars were murderers all the time!" He glanced over at Red. "I was thinking ... perhaps Elaine would like to segue into some acting roles? Instead of working behind the scenes, I mean. The troupe has really taken a hit, you see. Under the circumstances."

Red sighed. "I'm sure she'd love to, if we can work out a babysitter for practices." He muttered under his breath to Miles, "Might keep Mama too busy to do any crime-fighting. And, actually, Elaine from trying to do something crafty. She's not necessarily gifted in arts and crafts. Bless her heart."

"And perhaps ... I hope it's not too much of an imposition, but I'm already looking ahead of our next production and I think we need to do a very basic, all-American kind of thing. And, ah, cheap, of course. I was wondering, Miss Myrtle, if I could perhaps borrow some of your gnomes? For the set, you know."

Myrtle beamed at him. "Finally someone who recognizes my gnomes' artistic value."

Red laughed. "Mr. Toucan, I will personally deliver the gnomes *myself*. As many as you'd like."

Mr. Toucan added, "And I believe I owe you a debt of gratitude, Miss Myrtle."

"For ridding your theater of murderers? It's all in a day's work, Mr. Toucan," said Myrtle.

"Actually, well, yes, for that, too. But also for suggesting Tippy Chambers. She's created the Friends of the Theater foundation and is planning a big fundraiser. She's ensuring that there *is* a next production. And I owe it all to you for thinking of it."

Myrtle felt the day couldn't be any better at this point.

Lt. Perkins closed his notebook. "Well, I think we're done here. Miss Myrtle, good working with you again. Mr. Toucan, I'll fill you in if you can wait for a couple of minutes after I finish making a call to the station. I believe I need to also inform you of some possible petty theft."

Mr. Toucan nodded slowly. "Oh. Oh dear. Well, thanks." His glance took in the scattered squash and the push pole and lashing that weren't in their correct places. "Oh my."

Myrtle stood up from the folding chair she'd been sitting on and Red said, "I suppose you walked here, Mama. In waning daylight. With a bag of squash." Myrtle gave him a stubborn look and he sighed. "I'll drive you home and then I've got to get back to the station. Looks like it's going to be another late night."

Miles said, "I'll drive you back, Myrtle. That will save Red a trip."

"Thank you," she said.

They strolled out the back door and Myrtle glanced down at the bottom of the stairs. "Well, would you look at that?"

Cady was still at the theater, apparently waylaid by Skip. He had his arm protectively around her and was listening intently to whatever she was saying.

"I'd never have put those two together," said Miles under his breath.

"I suppose a common interest? The theater has brought them together," murmured Myrtle. "Or murder."

The two glanced up at them as they came down the stairs. Skip said, "I heard the sirens and came over. Cady has been filling me in on what happened." He smiled warmly at Cady. "Actually, she's had to tell me more than once for me to be able to take it all in. Are you all right, Miss Myrtle?" he asked.

"Right as rain," said Myrtle with a sniff. "Blaine didn't realize who he was dealing with."

Cady pulled Myrtle to one side as Skip quizzed Miles about what he knew. Cady said, "What do you think about Skip? I can't believe I never realized how really sweet he is. He was so worried about me!"

They looked over at Skip, listening carefully as Miles was describing the scene inside with some degree of animation.

Myrtle said, "At least we know Skip isn't a murderer. And that he appears to care about you. I think that sounds like a great starting point."

Cady nodded and smiled as Skip held out a hand to her. She slipped her hand inside his and they went in to see Mr. Toucan.

Myrtle climbed into Miles's car. "Now I'm tired. You were sleepy earlier and Red was clearly sleeping when I called him to the theater. But I was okay until now."

"The adrenaline is gone," said Miles succinctly as he drove toward Myrtle's house. "Speaking of our long day—did you see the paper at the beginning of it?"

"No. I was too busy trying to figure out my funeral attire. Why?"

Miles said, "I was busy, too. But this afternoon after I'd put away the groceries, I thought I'd work on the crossword a few minutes. Sometimes it makes me sleepy. Anyway, on the crossword page, I saw the horoscope." He patted a neatly folded paper that was tucked into the center console of his car.

Myrtle pulled it out and Miles added, "I thought you said you were editing Wanda's horoscopes."

"Are you kidding? Of *course* I am. Even Sloan would be appalled by her grammar and spelling. I edited it and emailed it to Sloan yesterday afternoon. Why?" She started unfolding the paper.

"I guess Wanda must have gone to the *Bugle* and changed the horoscope you'd edited," said Miles, pulling into Myrtle's driveway. "Take a look at your horoscope for the day."

Myrtle peered at the Libra section. It said: *Squash is gud fer you*.

About the Author:

Elizabeth writes the Southern Quilting mysteries and Memphis Barbeque mysteries for Penguin Random House and the Myrtle Clover series for Midnight Ink and independently. She blogs at ElizabethSpannCraig.com/blog , named by Writer's Digest as one of the 101 Best Websites for Writers. Elizabeth makes her home in Matthews, North Carolina, with her husband. She is the mother of two.

Sign up for Elizabeth's free newsletter to stay updated on its release:

https://elizabethspanncraig.com/newsletter/

Other Works by the Author:

Myrtle Clover Series in Order:
Pretty is as Pretty Dies
Progressive Dinner Deadly
A Dyeing Shame
A Body in the Backyard
Death at a Drop-In
A Body at Book Club
Death Pays a Visit
A Body at Bunco
Murder on Opening Night
Cruising for Murder
A Body in the Trunk
Cleaning is Murder
Edit to Death
Southern Quilting Mysteries in Order:
Quilt or Innocence
Knot What it Seams
Quilt Trip
Shear Trouble
Tying the Knot

Patch of Trouble

Fall to Pieces

Rest in Pieces

On Pins and Needles

Fit to be Tied (2019)

The Village Library Mysteries in Order (Debuting 2019):

Checked Out (2019)

Memphis Barbeque Mysteries in Order (Written as Riley Adams):

Delicious and Suspicious

Finger Lickin' Dead

Hickory Smoked Homicide

Rubbed Out

And a standalone "cozy zombie" novel: Race to Refuge, written as Liz Craig

This and That

I love hearing from my readers. You can find me on Facebook as Elizabeth Spann Craig Author, on Twitter as elizabethscraig, on my website at elizabethspanncraig.com, and by email at elizabethspanncraig@gmail.com. Thanks so much for reading my book...I appreciate it. If you enjoyed the story, would you please leave a short review on the site where you purchased it? Just a few words would be great. Not only do I feel encouraged reading them, but they also help other readers discover my books. Thank you!

Interested in having a character named after you? In a preview of my books before they're released? Or even just your name listed in the acknowledgments of a future book? Visit my Patreon page at https://www.patreon.com/elizabethspanncraig .

I have Myrtle Clover tote bags, charms, magnets, and other goodies at my Café Press shop: https://www.cafepress.com/cozymystery

If you'd like an autographed book for yourself or a friend, please visit my Etsy page.

I'd also like to thank some folks who helped me put this book together. Thanks most of all to my family, especially Coleman, Riley, and Elizabeth Ruth. Many thanks to Judy Beatty for editing. Thanks to my mother, Beth Spann, for her suggestions and support. A special thanks to Karri Klawiter for her cover design. My thanks to Amanda Arrieta for her insightful beta reading. And thanks, as always, to the writing community for its support and encouragement.

Printed in Great Britain
by Amazon

75568178R00149